William Lloyd Garrison

The new

William Lloyd Garrison

The new

ISBN/EAN: 9783744785556

Printed in Europe, USA, Canada, Australia, Japan

Cover: Foto ©Andreas Hilbeck / pixelio.de

More available books at **www.hansebooks.com**

ANTI-SLAVERY TRACTS. No. 4. New Series.

THE

NEW "REIGN OF TERROR"

IN THE

SLAVEHOLDING STATES,

FOR

1859-60.

NEW YORK:

PUBLISHED BY THE AMERICAN ANTI-SLAVERY SOCIETY.

1860.

PREFACE.

"There exists," says the New York *Tribune*, "at this moment, throughout the Southern States, an actual Reign of Terror. No Northern man, whatever may be his character, his opinions, or his life, but simply because he is a Northern man, can visit that region without the certainty of being subjected to a mean espionage over all his actions, and a rigid watchfulness over all his expressions of opinions; with the risk of personal indignity, and danger even to life and limb. This mortifying necessity of submission to a contemptible despotism, or suffering the penalty of any assertion of an independent and manly spirit, is confined to no condition of life, but is enforced upon every visitor, whether he be a poor mechanic like Powers, who hammers stone for a living, a merchant's clerk like Crangale, who is paid with imprisonment for asking the settlement of a just debt, a peddler who sells books as harmless as a dictionary, or a Member of Congress, who, for words spoken in debate, may be, by the bludgeon of a bully, incapacitated for the rest of his life for following any honorable or useful career. Nor is it necessary even to cross Mason and Dixon's line to come under this degrading compulsion. Northern merchants who sell goods for Southern consumption are called upon to square their opinions according to the plantation standard, and any recusancy on their part is visited with the discipline of the loss of trade. Editors of petty Southern newspapers hardly capable of forming an intelligent notion upon any subject, and quite incapable of writing two consecutive sentences of even tolerable English, form their Black Lists and White Lists, and compel the obedience and subsidy of large commercial houses of a great, and wealthy, and powerful city, a thousand miles distant. And, worst of all, this state of things seems accepted rather as in the natural order of events, than as a monstrous growth of an insolent tyranny on the one hand, and the subserviency of an infinitely mean, and sordid, and peddling poltroonery on the other.

And here is its latest development. A morning paper of yesterday publishes 'a card,' signed 'James P. Hambleton, editor of the *Southern Confederacy*.' The Black List of the *Confederacy* had included the name of Davis, Noble & Co., No. 87 Chambers street, and the purpose of the card is to exonerate this firm from the charge implied in that publication, the

editor being now satisfied, on ' the best evidence, that the aforesaid firm
are true, constitutional men, having never been tainted with any of the
Anti-Slavery *isms* of the day, either directly or indirectly, and that we
hereby recommend them to their former patrons at the South, as a concern
in every respect deserving their continued patronage and support.' We
neither know nor care what the evidence may be which has produced this
change — whether it be a suit of clothes, a pair of shoes, a hat, a bill of
dry goods, a bill of wet goods, or fifty dollars in current bills — the fact
itself is enough. The disgraceful fact is enough that this Hambleton is at
this moment in New York; that he is, while we write, making a round of
calls upon tradesmen, receiving sometimes money, sometimes goods, and always the evidence of the most despicable subserviency, on condition that
he will certify to that fact; and that nowhere, among all these tradesmen
— men who on Sunday go to church, who are not hissed when they appear
in public, who look their wives in the face, who meet their children un-
abashed, who go into the streets by daylight — men, moreover, whose legs
have the ordinary muscular development, whose boots have the ordinary
thickness, to all whose stores there is a front door — have not one of them,
as yet, indignantly ejected Mr. James P. Hambleton from their premises!
We honestly and sincerely think that this is a fact not to be laughed at,
but one which demands our most serious consideration."

Let us suppose the tables to be turned; suppose there existed here a little
of the spirit of '76, such as our fathers manifested in their treatment of
the tories at that time, and we should catch, and tar and feather, every
slaveholder coming into the North, by way of retaliation, and to show
our jealous appreciation of the sacred cause of freedom — how long would
" our glorious Union" hold together? How many victims would be subjected to *Northern* Lynch law, before the South would bring this matter to
a head? And yet, there are scores of Northern men so treated at the
South, — not one of them an Abolitionist, or in sympathy with their movement, — and the intelligence excites no popular indignation among us, and
scarcely elicits a comment from the press. In one half of the country,
there is, practically, no Constitution or Union now; there, all constitutional rights are ruthlessly violated in the persons of those who believe in the
Declaration of Independence and the Golden Rule; there, a bloody usurpation holds undisputed sway. And for such atrocities there is no remedy ;
at least, none is looked for, none even attempted. The submission to them,
on the part of the North, is as absolute as that exacted of the scourged and
cowering slaves on the plantation !

People of the North ! read and ponder the following record of the high-
handed measures and lawless deeds referred to, and decide the question,
— OF WHAT VALUE IS THE UNION?

THE NEW REIGN OF TERROR.

AUTHORISED VIOLATION OF THE MAILS.

RICHMOND, Va., Nov. 28th, 1859.

A Postmaster in the county of Doddridge, in this State, wrote recently to Gov. Wise, asking information as to what disposition he should make of such incendiary newspapers as the New York *Tribune*, and others of that stamp from Ohio, received in that county. The Governor referred the matter to John Randolph Tucker, Esq., the Attorney-General for this State, and probably the ablest constitutional lawyer in the Commonwealth, for his opinion. Mr. Tucker examined the subject very carefully, and, as will be seen by his opinion, which I herewith transmit, disposed *satisfactorily* of the apparent conflict of jurisdiction between the State and Federal authorities involved in this question : —

RICHMOND, Nov. 26th, 1859.

SIR, — The question is submitted to me for an opinion as to the effect of the law of Virginia upon the distribution of mail matter when it is of an incendiary character. A newspaper, printed in the State of Ohio, propagating abolition doctrines, is sent to a person through a post office in Virginia. What is the duty of the Postmaster in the premises ?

The law of Virginia (Code of Va., chap. 198, sec. 24) provides that " If a Postmaster or Deputy Postmaster know that any such book or writing (referring to such as advise or incite negroes to rebel or make insurrection, or inculcate resistance to the right of property of masters in their slaves) has been received at his office in the mail, he shall give notice thereof to some Justice, who shall inquire into the circumstances, and have such book or writing burned in his presence; if it appear to him that the person to whom it was directed subscribed therefor, knowing its character, or agreed to receive it for circulation to aid the purposes of abolitionists, the Justice shall commit such person to jail. If any Postmaster or Deputy Postmaster violate this section, he shall be fined not exceeding two hundred dollars."

This law is obligatory upon every Postmaster and Deputy Postmaster in the Commonwealth; and it is his duty, upon being aware that such book or writing is received at his office, to notify a Justice of the fact, that he may take the proceedings prescribed in the section quoted.

This State law is entirely constitutional, and does not, properly considered, conflict with the Federal authority in the establishment of post offices and post roads. This Federal power to transmit and carry mail matter does not carry with it the power to publish or to circulate. This last is a great State power, reserved and absolutely necessary to be maintained as a security to its citizens and to their rights. If the States had surrendered this power, it would, in these important particulars, have been at the mercy of the Federal authorities.

With the transmission of the mail matter to the point of its reception, the Federal power ceases. At that point, the power of the State becomes exclusive. Whether her citizens shall receive the mail matter, is a question exclusively for her determination. Whatever her regulation upon the subject, is for her decision alone, and no one can gainsay it. Her sovereign right to make it closes the door to cavil and objection.

It is true the Postmaster is an officer of the Federal Government, but it is equally true he is a citizen of the State. By taking the Federal office, he cannot avoid his duty as a citizen; and the obligation to perform the duty of his office cannot absolve him from obedience to the laws of his Commonwealth, nor will they be found to conflict. The State, in the case supposed, holds the hand of her citizen from receiving what is sent to him, and takes it herself. No citizen has the right to receive an invitation to treason against the commands of his State, and her law forbidding it and commanding it to be burned, refers to the right of the citizen to receive, not to the right of the Federal power to transmit and carry mail matter intended for him, which he does not receive, only because the law of the State forbids it.

I have no hesitation in saying that any law of Congress, impairing directly or indirectly this reserved right of the State, is unconstitutional, and that the penalty of the State law would be imposed upon a Postmaster offending against it, though he should plead his duty to obey such unconstitutional act of Congress.

If there be a conflict, therefore, between the postal regulations of Congress and this law of Virginia, it is because the former have transcended their true constitutional limits, and have trenched upon the reserved rights of the State. In such a case the citizen, though a Postmaster, must take care to obey the legitimate authority, and will not be exempt from the penalty of the State law by reason of any obligation to perform the duties of a Federal office, which are made to invade the reserved jurisdiction of the State in matters involving her safety and her peace.

It is eminently important that the provisions of the law in question should be rigidly adhered to by all the Postmasters in the State, and that the Justices to whose notice the matter may be brought should firmly execute the law, whenever a proper case presents itself for their decision.

With high respect, your obedient servant,

J. R. TUCKER.

For the Governor.

LETTER FROM THE POSTMASTER-GENERAL.

POST OFFICE DEPARTMENT, Dec. 5th, 1859.

SIR, — I am in receipt of your letter of the 2d inst., in which, after referring to the opinion of the Attorney-General of Virginia sustaining the constitutionality of the statute of that State, denouncing, under heavy penalties, the circulation of books, newspapers, pamphlets, &c., tending to incite the slave population to insurrection, you ask to be instructed as to your duty in reference to such documents, should they be received through the mails for distribution at the post office of which you have charge.

The statute alluded to is in the following words : —

SEC. 23. If a free person write, print, or cause to be written or printed, any book or other writing- with intent to advise or incite negroes in this State to rebel or make insurrection, or inculcating resistance to the right of property of masters in their slaves, or if he shall, with intent to aid the purposes of any such book or writing, knowingly circulate the same, he shall be confined in the Penitentiary, not less than one nor more than five years.

SEC. 24. If any Postmaster or Deputy Postmaster know that any such book or other writing has been received at his office in the mail, he shall give notice thereof to some Justice, who shall inquire into the circumstances, and have such book or writing burned in his presence; if it appear to him that the person to whom it was directed subscribed therefor, knowing its character, or agreed to receive it for circulation to aid the purposes of Abolitionists, the Justice shall commit such person to jail. If any Postmaster or Deputy Postmaster violate this section, he shall be fined, not exceeding two hundred dollars.

The point raised by your inquiry is, whether this statute is in conflict with the act of Congress regulating the administration of this Department, which declares that "if any Postmaster shall unlawfully detain in his office any letter, package, pamphlet or newspaper, with the intent to prevent the arrival and delivery of the same to the person or persons to whom such letter, package, pamphlet or newspaper may be addressed or directed, in the usual course of the transportation of the mail along the route, he shall, on conviction thereof, be fined in a sum not exceeding five hundred dollars, and imprisoned for a term not exceeding six months, and shall moreover be forever thereafter incapable of holding the office of Postmaster in the United States."

The question thus presented was fully decided by Attorney-General Cushing in the case of the Yazoo City post office. (Opinions of Attorney-Generals, vol. 8, 489.) He there held that a statute of Mississippi, in all respects analogous to that of Virginia as cited, was not inconsistent with the act of Congress quoted, prescribing the duties of Postmasters in regard to the delivery of mail matter, and that the latter, as good citizens, were bound to yield obedience to such State laws.

You are referred to the luminous discussion of the case for the arguments urged by that distinguished civilian in support of the conclusion at which he arrived. The judgment thus pronounced has been cheerfully acquiesced in by this Department, and is now recognized as one of the guides of its administration. The authority of Virginia to enact such a law rests upon that right of self-preservation which belongs to every government and people, and which has never been surrendered, nor indeed can it be. One of the most solemn constitutional obligations imposed on the Federal Government is that of protecting the States against "insurrection" and "domestic violence"—of course, none of its instrumentalities can be lawfully employed in inciting, even in the remotest degree, to this very crime, which involves in its train all others, and with the suppression of which it is specially charged. You must, under the responsibilities resting upon you as an officer and as a citizen, determine whether the books, pamphlets, newspapers, &c., received by you for distribution, are of the incendiary character described in the statute; and if you believe they are, then you are not only not obliged to deliver them to those to whom they are addressed, but you are empowered and required, by your duty to the State of which you are a citizen, to dispose of them in strict conformity to the provisions of the law referred to. The people of Virginia *may not only forbid the introduction and dissemination of such documents within their borders, but, if brought there in the mails, they may, by appropriate legal proceedings, have them destroyed.* They have the same right to extinguish firebrands thus impiously hurled into the midst of their homes and altars, that a man has to pluck the burning fuse from a bombshell which is about to explode at his feet.

Very respectfully, your obedient servant,

J. HOLT.

Mr. CHARLES A. ORTON, Postmaster at Falls Church, Va.

1*

POST OFFICE, LYNCHBURG, Va., Dec. 2d, 1859.

MR. HORACE GREELEY — SIR, — I hereby inform you that I shall not, in future, deliver from this office the copies of the *Tribune* which come here, because I believe them to be of that incendiary character which are forbidden circulation alike by the laws of the land, and a proper regard for the safety of society. You will, therefore, discontinue them.

Respectfully,

R. H. GLASS, P. M.

———

LIFE IN VIRGINIA. — A private letter from a Postmaster in Virginia, whose locality we dare not indicate, for fear of exposing him to mob violence, says: —

"We are in the midst of a Reign of Terror here. There is no certainty that letters duly mailed will not be opened on their way. All men of Northern birth now here are under *surveillance* by the so-called Vigilance Committee; and any one suspected of thinking slavery less than divine is placed under care. Those who have been taking the New York *Tribune* are objects of especial ban. A company of ten came into the office last Monday, and gave notice that I must not give out any more *Tribunes* to the subscribers here. The law of Virginia punishes by fine and imprisonment a Postmaster who gives out what are denounced as incendiary journals. The law of the United States punishes by fine and imprisonment, and further incapacitates from ever holding the office again, any Postmaster who shall withhold or refuse to deliver any paper sent to a regular subscriber at his office. So here I am in a pretty fix."

———

John C. Underwood, Esq., writing to Horace Greeley under date of "Occoquan, Prince William Co., Va., Dec. 21st, 1859," says — "There are some ten or twelve copies of the *Tribune* taken at this office, and the Postmaster refuses to deliver them to the subscribers! The Attorney-General of this State has pronounced them incendiary!"

HARPER'S MAGAZINE AND WEEKLY PROSCRIBED. — The *North Carolinian*, of Fayetteville, N. C., says: "We notice these periodicals upon our streets as numerous as ever, after it is ascertained that G. W. Curtis, one of the editors, is an infamous Abolitionist, and that one of the Harpers has given a large sum of money to the Brown sympathizers. Should these papers be allowed to circulate so profusely in our midst? We notice that his Honor, Judge Saunders, put a stop to the sale of these papers in Raleigh. We would like to know why they are not stopped here. Are we to see these Abolition sheets upon our street without a word of rebuke?"

MORE MOB SPIRIT. — On Friday evening, of last week, the editor of the *Peninsular News*, a most excellent anti-slavery paper, published at Milford, Delaware, received an intimation that a mob of violent men were making arrangements to attack his office, and destroy the press and type. The matter having leaked out, several substantial citizens of Milford repaired to the office, and volunteered to assist in its defence. The mob collected around the office in considerable numbers, but concluded that the movement was not popular enough in that town, and retired. The attempt has created much indignation among the best portion of the citizens of Milford, who know that the *News* is telling the truth about slavery, and that mobs and all the efforts of Slavery-ridden Democrats will not stop the spread of such truths as it publishes.

Norris F. Stearns, of Greenfield, Mass., a straight-out Democrat, was recently driven from Georgetown, S. C., where he went to sell maps, because he was from the North; and a subscriber to the Greenfield *Gazette*, in Georgia, has been obliged to discontinue his subscription on account of the anti-Northern feeling there. Nothing sectional in these and similar incidents, of course! The South is composed of *national* men!

EXPULSIONS OF CITIZENS OF KENTUCKY.

The Cincinnati *Commercial* of Dec. 31st, says that thirty-six persons arrived in that city from Kentucky, on the 30th, having been warned to leave the State for the crime of believing slavery to be a sin. They are from Berea and vicinity in Madison county, neighbors, co-workers and friends of Rev. John G. Fee.

Among the exiles are Rev. J. A. R. Rogers, principal of a flourishing school at Berea, and his family; J. D. Reed and family; John S. Hanson and family. Mr. Hanson is a native of Kentucky, and a hard-working, thrifty man. He had recently erected a steam saw-mill, and owns five hundred acres of land in Madison county, Ky. The Rev. J. F. Boughton; E. T. Hayes and S. Life, carpenters; A. H. Toney, a native of Tennessee; John Smith, a native of Ohio, a farmer, who has lived in Kentucky some years. Mr. Smith is described by Mr. Fee as a gray-haired father, a man of prayer, indeed of eminent piety and usefulness. More than half of the exiles are natives of Southern States, and several are native Kentuckians. The only offence charged against any of them is that of entertaining abolition sentiments.

The movement for expelling these men arose from the excitement of the John Brown foray. At a pro-slavery meeting held at Richmond, at which, according to the Kentucky papers, the "oldest, most respectable, and law-abiding citizens were in attendance," it was resolved on the ground of "self-preservation," to appoint a committee of sixty-five, to remove from among them J. G. Fee, J. A. R. Rogers, and so many of their associates as in their best judgment the peace and safety of society may require. The committee were instructed to perform this duty "deliberately and humanely as may be, but most effectually." At the meeting, a letter of J. A. R. Rogers was read, inviting any gentleman of the county who, from rumor or otherwise, has formed an unfavorable opinion of the community of Berea, to visit it, and learn its true character. He says: —

"We do not profess to be faultless, but hope that the compliments for industry, probity and good citizenship, that have been paid us by those of the first rank in the county for wealth and influence, who have made our acquaintance, may be more and more deserved.

It is universally known that most of us, in common with Washington and a host of others, whom we all delight to honor, believe that slavery is a moral and political evil; that it is the duty and privilege of those holding slaves to free them at the earliest consistent moment, and in such a way as to promote the general good; and that complexion is not the true test for the regard or privileges that should be extended to a man. We believe, too, that moral and political means only should be used to remove slavery. Insurrection finds no favor here. Brother Fee never has, and if his words be known, I doubt not does not now give the least countenance to the use of force in hastening the end of slavery.

Hoping that our confidence may be fully and intelligently placed in Him who once was despised, but is now exalted to be a Prince and Saviour, I remain yours respectfully."

The committee were ordered to carry out the designs of the meeting within ten days, and Mr. Rogers thus describes the warning which he received : —

"He was in his cottage, when a summons for him to appear was heard. On going to the door, he discovered an imposing cavalcade, sixty-five well-mounted men being drawn up in warlike array. He was informed that he had ten days in which to leave the State. This was on the 23d of December. He told them that he had not consciously violated any law of the Commonwealth, and that, if he had unconsciously done so, he would be most happy to be tried according to law. He was informed that they did not know that he had violated any law, but that his principles were incompatible with the public peace, and that he must go. The charge against him was abolitionism — the penalty, expulsion from the State.

No harsh or personally disrespectful language was used. He was even told with much courtesy of word and manner, that he was esteemed as a gentleman, but his presence was offensive on account of his principles. They laid it down as an axiom, that such sentiments as he entertained were not to be tolerated by a slaveholding people—that abolition doctrines and slaveholding were not to be permitted together — that one or the other must go under, and that they were resolved he and his friends must go. They warned him peaceably, but any amount of force necessary to carry out the objects of the Richmond meeting would be unhesitatingly employed. They appeared now in peace, but if he did not heed the warning, they would re-appear for war."

The committee represented the wealth and respectability of Madison county, and was sustained for the most part by public sentiment. There were, however, quite a number of slaveholders residing in the vicinity, who were opposed to the proceedings of the higher law pro-slavery zealots.

The *Commercial* in continuation says : —

"A paper was circulated through the county for signatures, (over seven hundred of which were obtained,) endorsing the action taken by the Rich-

mond meeting, and expressive of the sense of the community, that the
abolitionists must be driven out. Those who had charge of this paper do
not seem to have had any objections to procuring signatures under false
pretences. A slaveholder was called on, and asked whether he approved
of the John Brown foray. Of course he said he did not. He was then
told to sign that paper. He did so, and when he found out the nature of
the document, and the real object of obtaining his signature, he was indignant, and wished to withdraw his name, but was deterred by threats from
doing so. No signatures to this paper were obtained in the immediate
vicinity of Berea, except in this way, a fact which indicates that the neighbors of the Free Soilers did not think them dangerous citizens.

There were some friends of the proscribed persons willing to risk every-
thing and stand by them, but knowing that fighting would be unavailing,
they concluded to be without the State within the time assigned for their
removal. And they are consequently exiles in our midst, and afford a lesson of the nature of the intolerant despotism of the Slave Power, which
should not be lost upon those who are solicitous as to the *status* of the
American States."

Before leaving, they made an appeal to Gov. Magoffin for
protection, and a committee of them presented the Governor
the following petition : —

To His Excellency the Governor of the State of Kentucky :

We, the undersigned, loyal citizens and residents of the State of Kentucky and county of Madison, do respectfully call your attention to the
following facts : —

1. We have come from various parts of this and adjoining States to this
county, with the intention of making it our home, have supported ourselves
and families by honest industry, and endeavored to promote the interest of
religion and education.

2. It is a principle with us to "submit to every ordinance of man for
the Lord's sake; unto governors as unto them that are sent by Him for the
punishment of evil-doers, and the praise of them that do well," and in accordance with this principle, we have been obedient in all respects to the
laws of this State.

3. Within a few weeks, evil and false reports have been put into circulation, imputing to us motives, words and conduct calculated to inflame the
public mind, which imputations are utterly false and groundless. These
imputations we have publicly denied, and offered every facility for the fullest investigation, which we have earnestly but vainly sought.

4. On Friday, the 23d inst., a company of sixty-two men, claiming to
have been appointed by a meeting of the citizens of our county, without
any shadow of legal authority, and in violation of the Constitution and
laws of the State and United States, called at our respective residences and
places of business, and notified us to leave the county and State, and be
without this county and State within ten days, and handed us the accom-
panying document, in which you will see that, unless the said order be
promptly complied with, there is expressed a fixed determination to remove
us by force.

In view of these facts, which we can substantiate by the fullest evidence,
we respectfully pray that you, in the exercise of the power vested in you

by the Constitution, and made your duty to use, do protect us in our rights as loyal citizens of the Commonwealth of the State of Kentucky.

J. A. R. ROGERS,	SWINGLEHURST LIFE,
J. G. HANSON,	JOHN SMITH,
I. D. REED,	E. T. HAYES,
JAS. S. DAVIS,	CHAS. E. GRIFFIN,
JOHN F. BOUGHTON,	A. G. W. PARKER,

W. H. TORREY.

BEREA, Madison Co., Ky., Dec. 24th, 1859.

Gov. Magoffin, says the *Commercial*, received the bearers of the petition (Reed and Hayes) courteously, and advised them, for the sake of preserving the peace of the State, to leave it! He said that the public mind was deeply moved by the events in Virginia, and that until the excitement subsided, their presence in the State would be dangerous, and he could not engage to protect them from their fellow-citizens who had resolved that they must go.

He promised them security while taking their departure, and that their property should be protected. They say that, for the most part, they were treated politely by those who have driven them from their homes, and they have hopes that presently the people of Kentucky will take a sober thought, and allow them to return to their several places of abode and accustomed avocations.

It is certainly not a light matter to drive out of a State men who build steam saw-mills, improve farms, keep schools, and labor faithfully as ministers of the Gospel, and who give no provocation to any in any way — who offend against no law — who make no war upon society — and who merely hold that slavery is a sin, and teach that it should come to an end in God's own good time. The steam-mill of Mr. Hanson was doing well until he was constrained to abandon it. The school of Mr. Rogers was in a flourishing condition, having nearly a hundred pupils during the last term, a great portion of them the children of slaveholders. Kentucky cannot afford to drive beyond her borders the men who build mills and academies.

The exiles seem in good spirits. They do not indulge even in unkind words about those who have made them homeless. They seem to be divided in opinion as to their course in future. They all hope to go back to Old Kentucky, and live, labor, and die on her soil. Some fear they cannot go back, and think of looking out for employment in the free States; and they have vague ideas of appealing for protection in their rights and immunities as citizens to the Federal Government.

———

LETTER FROM REV. JOHN G. FEE.

The following is an extract from a letter of Mr. Fee to one of the Secretaries of the American Missionary Association, dated Germantown, Bracken County, Ky., Jan. 25th: —

"I am enduring a great trial. The floods come over me. I am again to be driven out, by a more overwhelming force than was in Madison county. Last Monday, it was supposed there came from eight hundred to a thousand people at the county seat. With almost unanimous rush, the mass gathered from the two counties, (I am near the Mason county line,) and resolved to drive me out. Some ten or twelve days are given us to leave. A committee of one hundred men are appointed to come, and warn us to go. I have sought counsel of the Lord, and of friends. There can be no human protection. I am to be driven out from one of the best communities in the State.

A few days since, I went to Germantown, to talk with the leading influential citizens. I desired to meet them face to face to talk over the positions I assume, and the evils of mob violence. Brother Humlong, a man of true excellence, went with me.

We called, and talked freely with many. A physician, of commanding position in society, speaking of the people of Bethesda, friends of the Church, said, "I wish to Heaven all Kentucky was as that neighborhood." "The people," said he, "are industrious, quiet, upright citizens," and then repeated his wish! Now from this scene of thrift I must be driven, from relatives, from the dear brethren and sisters in the Church, and friends around. Also from the plan or prospect of building up churches in Kentucky, and, still harder, from the prospect of carrying to the people of Kentucky the only

Gospel that can save. I can understand, now, why the Saviour wept over Jerusalem, as he saw that people about to push the cup of Salvation from them. Oh, how I wish I could be with you, to tell the anguish of my heart for others, and to plan for the future! The giving up of property, home, all earthly considerations, are not so painful as the idea of giving up these churches, and the privilege of laboring directly with and for the people of Kentucky. How shall I go away, and give up this work? I cannot give it up. I must only change my place of labor for a time. For years I have had unceasing care and toil to get things so established here, that I could have a prospect of their standing. Other brethren have toiled for a like object. We hoped then to have rest of spirit, and to rejoice in that reaped growth, which we then expected to see when we should have lived down much of the opposition, and seen confidence secured. The rest has not yet come. The viper that now stings, has been nurtured into strength in the bosom of the denominations around us. Church and State have been warming into life that which is now poisoning their vitals, and ruthlessly destroying all law and order. The abomination of desolation is working. Can, oh, can this nation be roused to the work of exterminating this monster, Slavery? It can be done by means peaceful and legitimate, if Christians and philanthropists will only, at once, do their duty, in Church and State.

Brother Hanson, Griffin, Mallett, Holman, and Robinson, are ordered to leave here. Brother Davis (Rev. J. S. Davis, of Cabin Creek, Lewis Co.,) is also driven out. A tremendous meeting for that purpose preceded the one held here."

ANOTHER EXPULSION FROM KENTUCKY.

Some of the persons lately expelled from Berea, Madison County, Kentucky, having manifested an intention of taking up their abode in Bracken and Lewis Counties, strong manifestations of displeasure have been exhibited by a portion of the inhabitants of those localities. The excitement has been growing more intense for a week or two past, and at last found its vent in meetings, the proceedings of which we annex.

On Saturday, the 21st, a public meeting was held at Orangeburg, Mason County, where the following resolutions were passed : —

Whereas, Our fellow citizens of the county of Madison have recently expelled therefrom the Rev. John G. Fee — a radical Abolitionist and zealous agent and emissary of the Anti-Slavery Societies of the North — and many confederates in the dissemination of his principles, and the accomplishment of the illegal and dangerous purposes of his mission; be it, therefore,

1. Resolved, That we approve of the action of the citizens of Madison county, rendered, as we believe, necessary and justifiable by a proper regard for the protection of their property, and the safety and security of their families.

2. That no Abolitionist has a right to establish himself in the slaveholding community, and disseminate opinions and principles destructive of its tranquillity and safety.

3. That forbearance ought nor will not by us be extended to those persons who come hither with intent to, and who do actually interfere with our rights of property or domestic institutions. Our own peace, and the good of the slaves, alike demand their expulsion.

4. That Kentucky has never assailed, openly or covertly, the rights or institutions of the North, nor will she suffer, silently or unrepelled, any aggression upon those guaranteed to her, either by her own or that of the Constitution of the United States.

5. That we desire and demand to be "let alone," leaving our officious and philanthropic friends at the North and elsewhere to work out their personal and social "salvation with fear and trembling."

6. That the Rev. James S. Davis (a co-worker with the Rev. John G. Fee, and one of those expelled from Madison) is, as we understand, now resident on Cabin Creek, in Lewis County, Ky., and has, as we are informed, recently received for circulation a large number of "Helper's Compendium of the Impending Crisis of the South," a book, in the estimation of this meeting, dangerous in its spirit and tendencies. Be it, therefore, further resolved, That his presence and residence among us are highly objectionable, and that he be and is hereby advised and requested to remove from Kentucky, and that Charles Dimmitt, John R. Bean, James Francis, Samuel Ilord, James Ilise, Garrett Bradley, and Leonard Bean are hereby appointed a committee to inform Mr. Davis of the purpose and object of this meeting, and that he comply with said request within seven days next after the same is made him, or suffer the consequences of non-compliance therewith. Duty, safety, and the interest of the community compelling us, in the event of non-compliance, to resort to means alike painful to us and hazardous to him.

7. In case Mr. Davis does not leave, that the committee hereinbefore appointed call another public meeting to consider and determine what action shall be had in the premises.

8. That these proceedings be signed by the President and Secretary, and published in the Maysville papers.

On Monday, the 23d inst., a meeting was held at Brooksville, Bracken County, the proceedings of which we give below :

A meeting of the citizens of Bracken and Mason Counties, Kentucky, called for the purpose of considering the propriety of allowing John G. Fee & Co., and others of like character, to settle among us, was held at Brooksville, Bracken County, Ky., January 23d, 1860.

On motion of John H. Boude, Col. W. Orr was elected President, and Gen. Samuel Worthington and Rudolph Black, Vice Presidents. Arthur Fox, James W. Armstrong, and J. A. Kackley were appointed Secretaries.

On motion of Judge Joseph Doniphan, a Committee of twelve were appointed to draft resolutions expressive of the sense of this meeting. The following persons were appointed as said Committee: Dr. J. Taylor Bradford, Col. A. Bledsoe, W. P. Delty, Dr. John Coburn, Judge Joseph Doniphan, Isaac Reynolds, Henry Anderson, John F. French, A. J. Coburn, Robert Coleman, R. P. Dimmitt, and Col. A. Soward.

The Committee, through their Chairman, Judge Joseph Doniphan, presented the following resolutions, which were unanimously adopted : —

Whereas, John Gregs Fee and John G. Hanson, lately expelled from Madison County, Kentucky, are now in Bracken County, preparing to make it their home. And whereas, that both Fee and Hanson are enemies to the State, dangerous to the security of our lives and property, we, the citizens of Kentucky, deem it our duty to protect our lives and property from enemies at home as well as abroad, do now solemnly declare the said John G. Fee and John G. Hanson must, by the 4th day of February next, leave this county and State.

1. That we earnestly entreat them to do so without delay, but in the event of their failure to do so by that time, they shall do so, even should it require physical force to accomplish the end.

2. That J. B. Mullett, a school teacher in District No. 27, and Wyatt Robinson and G. R. Holeman, must leave this county and State at the same time; and in the event of their failing or refusing, they shall be expelled by force; and that for the purpose of carrying out these resolves, a Committee of fifty of our citizens be appointed to notify the said Hanson, Fee, Mallett, Robinson and Holeman of the action of this meeting, and said Committee be also empowered to give notice to any other persons of like character to leave the State, and report the same to the meeting to be held in Germantown on the 6th day of February next.

3. That Dr. J. Taylor Bradford, Chairman; Rudolph Black, W. H. Reynolds, Henderson Anderson, Jonathan Hedgecock, C. A. Soward, W. Orr, Sr., John W. Terhune, Washington Ward, Jesse Holton, John Taylor, J. W. Armstrong, James Booth, W. Winter, Marcus Ware, E. W. Chinn, R. S. Thomas, John M. Walton, R. P. Dimmitt, Wm. Dougherty, J. A. Kackley, John M. Pearl, Robt. Coleman, David Brooks, Thurman Pollock, Joseph

Doniphan, A. D. Moore, Riley Rout, D. R. Cinville, J. H. Murry, Sen., of Bracken; A. Killgore, Gen. Samuel Worthington, J. E. French, Benjamin Kirk, Chas. Gordon, Isaac Reynolds, Col. A. Bledsoe, James Y. Reynolds, Evan Lloyd, Dr. John A. Coburn, Jacob Slack, B. W. Woods, Sr., Gen. Samuel Foreman, A. J. Coburn, C. A. Lyon, Samuel Frazee, A. Fox, R. C. Lewis, John D. Lloyd, Thornton Norris, Thomas Worthington, J. W. Reynolds, J. G. Bacon, and A. Hargot, of Mason, shall compose that Committee. That said Committee, in the event of said Fee, Hanson, Mallett, Robinson, and Holeman, failing to remove, that then the Committee report the result to a meeting to be held in Germantown, Ky., on the 6th day of February next.

4. That we deprecate the use of a church, known as the Free Church, by Abolition preachers; and we now solemnly declare that we will resist, by all possible means, the occupying said church, by such incendiary persons.

5. That the Secretaries be requested to prepare copies of the proceedings of this meeting, and furnish, one each, to *The Mountain Democrat, The Richmond Messenger, The Augusta Sentinel, The Maysville Eagle,* and *The Maysville Express.*

The meeting then adjourned.   WILLIAM ORR, President.

ARTHUR FOX, JAMES W. ARMSTRONG, J. A. KACKLEY, Secretaries.

In accordance with the resolutions adopted at the Bracken county meeting, a Committee representing the organized mob proceeded on Thursday, the 25th inst., to the work assigned them, and notified Fee, Hanson, Mallett, Holeman, Robinson, Griggson, and Griffin that they must be without the State on or by the 4th of February next.

They assumed an astonishing amount of pomposity. Such was the power assumed by them, that they passed through the toll-gate, and informed the keeper that "this company paid no toll."

They first met in Germantown, and proceeded in a body to the residence of Mr. John Humlong, and called for J. B. Mallett.

He came out within a few steps of the company, when the Chairman, Dr. Bradford, called out in a stern voice, as follows: "Walk this way, Mr. Mallett; don't have any fears, we don't intend to hurt you." Mr. Mallett replied, "No, he expected not; he was in the company of gentlemen, he supposed." Dr. Bradford read the resolutions, and asked, "Do you intend to leave?" Mr. Mallett replied that he had said he intended to do so.

Mr. Mallett asked the privilege of making a few remarks, but was told that the mob had no time to listen. Mr. Humlong asked, and was also denied this privilege. However, he made the inquiry, what was this for? They replied, for teaching incendiary and insurrectional sentiments. Mr. H. said he would say, to the contrary, the teaching had always been that of peace.

They then proceeded to G. G. Hanson's, and in the same pompous manner notified his son to leave.

Mr. J. G. Hanson endeavored to get a hearing, but to no purpose. In this mob were some of his relations.

They next called at Mr. Vincent Hamilton's, father-in-law of John G. Fee. Mr. Fee told them he had intended to leave, yet in their notice he recognized no right to require him to leave. He asked the mob to pause a moment, but the Chairman ordered them to proceed. He was previously told that he was smart enough to keep out of the hands of the law, and this was the only course to get him out. As one of the mob passed, Mr. Fee extended his hand and said:

" Do you approve of this action ? "

" Yes, I do," was the reply.

" Well," said Mr. Fee, " we took vows together in the same Church. I expected different things of you."

In that mob were school-mates, parents of school-mates, and life-long acquaintances.

From this they proceeded to the residence of Mr. John D. Gregg, where Mr. Holeman was stopping, in feeble health, and notified him, without a show of authority from any previous meeting, and ordered him, peremptorily, to be without the State by the 4th of February next.

J. G. Fee is a minister, and well known as being an earnest man, and esteemed by all who love and admire an honest man. J. G. Hanson is a citizen of Berea, from whence he had been driven, and was visiting at his father's. He had never been charged with a crime, unless it was his *honesty !* C. E. Griffin is also a Berean, and is noted for his quiet, peaceable character. Mr. Griffin is a quiet, unpretending laborer, and has always been noted for his amiable disposition. He is a poor man, and this blow is felt severely by him and his family. He is driven from the land of his nativity, the scenes of his childhood, and all his friends. G. R. Holeman has formerly been employed as a school-teacher, but has not been engaged in teaching this winter, on account of poor health. He is a native of Ohio. J. B. Mallett has taught

Locust Academy school for nearly three years. The school has the reputation of being one of the best in the country. Notwithstanding the school closed most abruptly, he received a certificate of respect, signed by the patrons of the institution. An enraged mob could not accuse, or sustain the accusation, that he was even aggressive in his teachings upon the subject of Slavery. Scholars who had attended the school six months, say they never heard the subject mentioned in the school. Yet he has ever acknowledge himself in the social circle to be an anti-slavery man. He is a native of New York State.

The people have for years sustained the reputation of being among the most honest and reliable men in the State. A prominent citizen and slaveholder said, "Would to God all Kentucky was like that neighborhood!"

The exiles left Germantown on Saturday morning. Eighteen, including women and children, made up the company of the expelled, and some of these persons arrived in this city last night. Legal advice was taken, prior to their leaving home, as to the best course to be pursued. It was found that they could only remain by resisting the mob, and this was not deemed advisable. It was therefore decided to withdraw quietly.

At Felicity, on Saturday night, a part of the exiles were present at a large meeting held in the M. E. Church.

The names of those who arrived here last night are as follows: C. E. Griffin and lady; the Rev. John G. Fee, J. G. Hanson, G. R. Holeman, J. B. Mallett, and Oliver Griggson. — *Cincinnati Daily Enquirer, Jan. 31st.*

———

A TAR AND FEATHERING CASE. — A Scotchman named Sandy Tate, having expressed himself rather too freely upon the slave question and Harper's Ferry affair, in the village of Salisbury, North Carolina, was recently seized by a mob, and tarred and feathered, after which he was placed upon a fence rail, and carried to a neighboring duck pond, where, in the presence of an immense throng of people, he was ducked until he recanted. Upon being released, the poor fellow took to his heels, and has never been seen since.

A PREACHER ARRESTED IN NORTH CAROLINA.

GREENSBORO', N. C., Dec. 26th, 1859.

On Friday, the 23d inst., Daniel Worth, a Wesleyan Methodist preacher, a native of this State, but who has been residing until within two years past in Indiana, where he was formerly a member of the Legislature of that State, was arrested by the Sheriff of this county on a charge of selling and circulating " Helper's Impending Crisis," and also of uttering language in the pulpit calculated to make slaves and free negroes dissatisfied with their condition, thereby offending against the laws of the State. He was brought before the magistrates of the town, and a partial hearing had, when the case was adjourned until the following afternoon at one o'clock, for the purpose of procuring the attendance of witnesses for the prosecution. The prisoner was taken to jail, bail having been refused by the magistrates.

On Saturday, at the appointed hour, the Court met. The examination was held in the old Court-House, which was crowded.

The prisoner had no counsel, but managed his own case. Messrs. Scott, Dick and McLean, of the Greensboro' bar, were engaged in the prosecution.

Over a dozen witnesses were examined, and it was conclusively proved that Worth had on many and various occasions uttered such sentiments in the pulpit against slavery as the State of North Carolina declared to be unlawful to be uttered. It was also proved by a witness that he (the witness) had purchased from Worth a copy of " Helper's Impending Crisis."

Worth acknowledged during the examination that he had been engaged in circulating Helper's book, and also a work on the " War in Kansas," but that he did not consider it any harm to circulate them ; that at first he did not intend to admit having circulated the former, but that he wanted to make them, as a lawyer would, bring evidence to substantiate the charge.

During the examination, various extracts were read from " Helper's Impending Crisis," some showing the *modus ope-*

randi by which slavery was to be got rid of in the South, and others pretending to give facts, all of which were commented on by the various counsel for the State.

It was also proved that Worth had, in the pulpit, on the Sabbath day, applied the most opprobrious epithets to the legislators of the State of North Carolina, saying that the laws ought not to be obeyed; that "they were made by a set of drunkards, gamblers and whoremongers."

The prosecution was opened by Wm. Scott, Esq., who, in his remarks, eloquently described the inhuman tendency of the doctrines ˙ ilcated and taught in this work of Helper's, which this traitor to the State of his birth had been engaged in circulating. He read many extracts from the book, and showed how grossly perverted were the facts pretended to be therein set forth — that they were base lies and calumnies on the South.

Robert P. Dick, Esq., made some highly effective and stirring remarks; he was glad that this case of Worth's had come up here in old Guilford county — a county that had the reputation of being an Abolition county; that a warrant had already been issued from Raleigh for this Daniel Worth, but that this was the best place for him to be tried, that the result of this examination might now go forth as a vindication from the foul aspersion cast upon it. He spoke of Helper as a traitor to the State that had once claimed him as a North Carolinian, adding that this man who sought, in his "Impending Crisis," to array the South against slavery, and bring about bloodshed and anarchy, and to desolate and lay waste the beautiful South, to dissolve the glorious Union, which had been given us by the wisdom of our forefathers, was obnoxious to the law under other criminal charges. He prayed and trusted that the Union would never be dissolved.

˙ Robert McLean, Esq., took up the question at issue. The very doctrines that the prisoner had been disseminating in his remarks from the pulpit, and which were contained in "Helper's Impending Crisis," which book he had been proved to have circulated, were at utter variance with the laws of the State of North Carolina, and it was upon this charge that he was now undergoing his examination. He read several extracts from Helper's work, commenting on them in a clear, forcible and telling manner. His remarks on the ways and means of abolishing slavery, as set forth in the "Impending Crisis," were very sarcastically commented on, and were much applauded by the large audience present.

He read from the "Impending Crisis," the names of Cheever, Chapin and Bellows, of the clergy of the North, as being engaged in the advocacy of those principles which were to dismember this Republic, and the name of the Rev. Daniel Worth as a Southern co-laborer.

It was extremely difficult to restrain the applause during the delivery of the remarks of all the legal gentlemen who spoke — the Court frequently interfering, and insisting upon order being observed.

Previous to the remarks of Robert McLean, Esq., the prisoner delivered his defence. He attempted to argue the evil of slavery, and to try and convince the Court that he was right in preaching against it. He was twice requested by the Court to stick to the point at issue; that they were not here to listen to a discussion on slavery, but to hear what he had to say in reply to the charges brought against him of violating the laws of North Carolina.

The prosecution requested the Court to let him go on.

The prisoner then continued his remarks at considerable length on Abolition, until the Court told him that it had listened long enough to that strain, and desired him to speak as to the charges brought against him. The prisoner then spoke as to his course having been consistent with his calling as a preacher and as a man; that when he heard there was a warrant out for his arrest, he had started for this place to surrender himself; that in his preaching and practice, he had only been doing what others in the State had long ago been doing unmolested; that he was a peace man and a Union man; that he sought not to dissever the Union; that he did not endorse all the sentiments contained in Helper's work; that he had formerly been a magistrate in this county; that he had been living in Indiana many years, and came back to North Carolina about two years since, to benefit the health of an invalid wife; that that wife had died, and he had married again, and had been engaged in preaching in several counties since; he was not conscious of having violated the laws of the State, either in his calling as a preacher, or as a circulator of "Helper's Impending Crisis."

2

The Court ordered him to find bail in $5,000 for his appearance at the next term of Court, and the same amount to keep the peace until that time. Bail for the first was offered, but up to the present time of writing, the other bail has not been obtained. It is said that should the prisoner be released on the above bail, he will be taken before his Honor, Judge Dick, who will refuse to take bail for him.

At the close of the examination, remarks were made by Ralph Gorrell, Esq., and Robert P. Dick, Esq., to the effect that the public mind was much excited by this examination, and that threats had been made as to a disposition of the prisoner; but that they would recommend the people to let the law take its course, and not to do any thing to militate against its authority, now that the prisoner was in its hands.

The Rev. Daniel Worth is a large, portly man, with a fine head, an intellectual and expressive countenance, and a large, commanding eye. He is fluent in speech, and the general style and manner of his speaking are calculated to win attention. He did not appear to be at all embarrassed or frightened at his position; on the contrary, he expressed his ideas and opinions with boldness and fearlessness. He complained to the Court of the unfitness of the jail for a prison, it being extremely cold weather, and no fire in the building; he had passed one night there, and was fully competent to express an opinion on the subject.

Mr. Worth was a man raised in this county, is sixty-five years old, and emigrated to Indiana and Ohio, and no doubt to Kansas. He was in the Legislature of the first-named State, acting as sub-chairman in the Convention that nominated Fremont for President.

I was glad to see that mob law was not exercised on him; but there is no doubt that the punishment prescribed for this offence by the laws of North Carolina will be fully meted out to him, which he and all others deserve who engage in such hellish work.

This man has been an eyesore to this community for eighteen months. Nothing but good feelings for the respectable family who bear his name has prevented him from incurring the same fate months ago. A clean sweep may now be expected by all who advocate such vile doctrines as those disseminated. Any man who is found with a volume of the

"Impending Crisis," or the sequel to it, will be held strictly accountable how he came by it. I am fully satisfied that if the course is persisted in which has already been attempted by our Northern Abolitionists, the North will suffer much in her trade with the Southern States, to say nothing of the political consequences attending it. It is as well to state that the punishment for the first offence of this kind under the statute laws of North Carolina is thirty-nine lashes; for the second, it is death, as meted out to John Brown and his fellow-associates at Harper's Ferry. — *Correspondence of the New York Herald.*

LETTER FROM A LADY TO AN OFFICER OF THE AMERICAN MISSIONARY ASSOCIATION.

GUILFORD COUNTY, N. C., Jan. 13th, 1860.

At present, we are circumstanced something like the children of Israel, when they started for the Land of Promise, pursued by Pharaoh and his host, with the Red Sea before them, and mountains on either hand. Still we hope to see the salvation of the Lord, relying on the arm of Jehovah for protection.

I suppose, ere this, you have seen some account of the Rev. D. Worth's arrest and commitment to prison, in Greensboro', Guilford County, N. C., charged with circulating incendiary books, &c., principally the "Impending Crisis," by Helper, which seems to be attracting more attention, at present, than all other books put together.

Brother Worth was arrested on the 23d of last month, had a preliminary trial before three magistrates on the 24th, which resulted in his commitment to prison to await further decision at the Spring Term of the Superior Court. There was great excitement during his trial; three lawyers appeared in behalf of the State; the prisoner pleaded his own cause in an able manner — his enemies themselves being judges. Since then, there have been five other arrests of citizens of this county for circulating "Helper," most of them under heavy bonds, but all admitted to bail except the first. The nature of the bonds required of him was considered unreasonable. The first was a bond of $5,000 for his appearance at the Spring Term, which was complied with; the other was $5,000 also, requiring him not to preach at all. This is not complied with, yet. Not content with the above, he was arrested again, in prison, and brought out yesterday before Judge Dick, and bound in the sum of $5,000 to appear at the Spring Term, in Randolph county, in March. His enemies seem determined to push the law to the furthest extremity, but the old veteran has been happy beyond description, and filled with joy unspeakable.

His keepers observe the strictest vigilance, not allowing even his wife to speak a word to him without witnesses being present; nor do they suffer him to write a word to any person, only what passes under their inspection. They made an attempt yesterday, during his trial, to deprive him of the means of writing at all; but finally concluded to let him have two or three sheets of paper at a time, by his giving an account to the Sheriff what disposition he made of it. One object seems to be to cut off all correspondence with friends, and indeed all the friends of liberty here must suffer likewise. They say that it is against the law to say slavery is wrong, and they have pronounced the woe; the decree has gone forth against all such offenders. I trust and believe there is a remnant who will trust and fear God more than man, even in this land of intolerance and usurpation; and I hope that all who love the Lord Jesus Christ in sincerity will remember us at the Throne of Grace, that we may be able to withstand all the fiery darts of the wicked; also, that our aged minister may be delivered from wicked and unreasonable men.

REV. DANIEL WORTH.—We have just heard from Mr. Worth, through his nephew, Rev. A. Worth. He is still in jail. His bail bonds would have been filed, but there were several Sheriffs hanging around the jail door from other counties, to arrest him as soon as he should come out of Greensboro' jail. His wife and friends are not permitted to visit him. His cell is wholly unsuitable for any person to live in.

His only bedding is a dirty pallet. The jail is strongly guarded. Some of the Quakers who were imprisoned have given bail, and are now out of jail. Several of them were leading and influential men. — *Randolph Co. (Ind.) Journal.*

———

WHIPPING A PREACHER. — The *Christian Luminary*, Cincinnati, January 12th, publishes an account, in three columns, of the whipping of Solomon M'Kinney. Mr. M'Kinney left Bloomfield, Iowa, last April, for Texas. He is about sixty years old, and has been a preacher thirty years. He is a Kentuckian, a Democrat, and understands slavery to be authorized by the Bible. While living in Texas, he boarded with Thomas Smith, a slaveholder, of Dallas Co., Texas, who was also a member of the church. Having been requested by T. Smith to preach on the relative duties of master and slave, Bro. M'Kinney did so, and reflected severely on the inhuman treatment servants sometimes receive. This resulted in the calling of a meeting, which, after having determined to "mobilize" all preachers of Mr. M'Kinney's type, appointed a committee to whip Mr. M'Kinney and a companion of his, both having previously been lodged in jail. Mrs. M'Kinney wanted to enter the jail with her husband, but was forced back by the mob, and compelled to await the result outside of the town. After dark, seven men came and opened the jail, and took the prisoners out; then, after divesting them of all their clothing, except shirt and pantaloons, they bound their wrists firmly with cords, and one held the cords while a second took a cowhide, and administered ten lashes; then another and another, till they had administered seventy lashes. The other, William Blunt, was next taken in hand, and served in the same way, receiving eighty lashes. The shirts of both were cut into ribbons by the raw hide. They were then unbound, and left to seek their company. Bruised, mangled, and bleeding, these wretched men staggered to the place where Mrs. M'Kinney was waiting for them. Their backs were one mass of clotted blood and gore, and bruised and mangled flesh.

Mr. Blunt, it appears, is a licensed minister of the Campbellite persuasion, and for twenty-four years has been a citizen of Green County, Wisconsin. The old Democrat has sent a long memorial to the Wisconsin Legislature on the subject of his experience among his Southern brethren, and asking redress for the wrongs and outrages received at the hands of the authorities of Texas. The Madison *State Journal* publishes the document, which created quite a flutter on the Democratic side of the Senate when read; and no wonder, for in Wisconsin the excoriated Reverend had distinguished himself by the blatant character of his advocacy of slavery. The *Journal* says: —

" He was particularly 'gifted' in the Biblical argument in favor of slavery; and, at Republican meetings, was wont to confront the speakers with long and flatulent speeches based upon Mosaic regulations. For more than thirty years, as he tells us in his memorial, the truth of which he attests under oath, he has voted the Democratic ticket.

" Last year he went down to Texas in quest of health, expecting a cordial welcome and a comfortable stay among the Democratic brethren, whose cause he had so faithfully advocated.

" The sequel is not calculated to quicken the ardor of Northern Democrats. The Rev. William Blunt was asked by an old friend and brother to fill some of his appointments; and, not knowing that his friend had been suspected of secretly cherishing Abolition sentiments, he acceded to the request. The result was, that he too fell under the suspicion of being an Abolitionist in disguise — he, the ardent, uncompromising Blunt, a Democrat of thirty years' standing — and therefore, as he relates with due particularity, he was set upon, arrested, his money taken from him, thrown into jail, taken out and treated to *eighty lashes*, and with other indignities and 'spurnings *a posteriori* not to be named,' told to leave that portion of this free and gel-lorious Republic forthwith without delay, which suggestion he proceeded to act upon with alacrity.

" In view of all the facts, he demands that the State of Wisconsin take such action as will enable him to obtain redress for the outrages perpetrated upon him."

DESPOTISM AND ESPIONAGE IN THE SOUTH.

We are continually receiving information, through private sources, from different parts of the South, which we shall from time to time publish, showing the fearful state of things now prevailing in all the Southern States, growing out of the popular excitement against the North and against Liberty. A Reign of Terror is prevailing. The despotism of Russia does not parallel the despotism of South Carolina. A stranger with a passport can freely travel in any part of the Czar's dominions; but no passport will guarantee safety to a Northern traveller between Richmond and New Orleans. It is no longer necessary that a man should speak against slavery to warrant his expulsion from a slave State. It is enough if he has simply been in the North, or sends his children to a Northern school, or buys his goods in New York or Boston. In almost every city, town and village south of the border slaveholding States, vigilance committees have been appointed, to put to inquisition every Northern man who makes his appearance in the place, whether as foe or friend. Even harmless young women, who have gone from Northern boarding-schools to be teachers of Southern children, have been waited upon by respectable and even clerical gentlemen, with the polite hint that the sooner they leave the State, the better for their safety. Our correspondents inform us that it is impossible to convey by description an adequate idea of the public sentiment in the extreme Southern States. The bitterness against the North is unparalleled. The common topic of talk is disunion, and the common threat of vengeance is to hang the Abolitionists. An Abolitionist, with the masses of the Southern people, is any man who does not live in a slaveholding State. If this definition were true, and the sentiment of the North were so unanimous in favor of freedom, the institution of slavery could not exist for half a year in the face of such an enlightened public opinion. We trust that the time may soon come when this shall be the strong and generous sentiment of all the free States. Such a sentiment would be a moral power for the overthrow of slavery, without violence or blood. The conduct of the South is exciting everywhere throughout the North a more intelligent, earnest and conscientious anti-slavery feeling. The frenzy of the Southern leaders, and of the Southern masses who follow and urge on their leaders, is only working the destruction of the system which they are seeking to defend. The providence of God was never more visible in human affairs than in the present state of the nation. We believe that the present excitement, while it will have the incidental evils common to all excitements, will in the end produce great good in the cause of the freedom of the enslaved.

We prefix to the array of facts which our correspondents have furnished us, the following brief but significant article from the Constitution of the United States, on the rights of citizens : —

"The citizens of each State shall be entitled to all the privileges and immunities of citizens in the several States."

The following incidents and statements will afford a commentary : —

The Northern newspapers have recently republished a brief paragraph from the Charleston *Mercury*, announcing, in a very nonchalant style, that a workman engaged in the State House, in Columbia, S. C., was recently seized by a mob, on account, as was alleged, of holding anti-slavery opinions, and that he received twenty-nine lashes, and was tarred and feathered, and escorted out of the State !

It took a very few lines to tell this story, according to the style of the Southern press; for it is a trait of Southern chivalry, first to practise cruelty, and then to suppress the facts.

We have seen this unfortunate man, and heard his story, and looked at his wounds. His name is James Power. He is an intelligent young man, about twenty-three years of age, a native of Wexford, Ireland, and a stone-cutter by trade. He went from Philadelphia to the South, and obtained employment in Columbia, where he had worked for nine months. The only opinion he ever expressed against slavery was that it caused a white laborer in the South to be looked upon as an inferior and degraded man. But this was enough ! The remark was reported to the Vigilance Committee, (composed of twelve members,) who immediately ordered the police to arrest him. He was seized two miles away from town, in attempting to escape. He was brought back, and put in a cell, where he remained for three days, during which time he was denied the use of pen and ink, and all communication with his friends outside.

At length he was taken before the Mayor. Four persons appeared and bore testimony to the remark which he had made. The evidence was conclusive. He was returned to prison, and kept locked up for six days. During this time, he was allowed only two scanty meals a day, and the food was carried to him by a negro. He was then taken out of jail in the custody of two marshals, who said to him : " You are so fond of niggers that we are going to give you a nigger escort."

He was led through the main street, amid a great crowd, hooting and yelling, the marshals compelling two negroes to drag him through the puddles and muddy places of the street, and of the State House yard ! As he was taken past the State House, three members of the Legislature, including the Speaker, stood looking on and laughing ! The crowd gradually increased, until it numbered several thousand persons, headed by a troop of horse.

After a march of three miles out of the city, to a place called "the Junction," the procession was stopped, and preparations were made for punishment. The populace cried, " Brand him ! " " Burn him ! " " Spike him to death ! " and made threats against his life by pointing pistols at his head, and flourishing sticks in his face.

The Vigilance Committee ordered him to strip himself naked, and forced a negro to assist in taking off the clothes. A cowhide was then put into the negro's hands, who was ordered to lay on thirty-nine lashes, (not twenty-nine, as reported,) and to draw blood with every stroke. Our informant describes the pain of this infliction as exceeding in severity any thing which he ever suffered before. His back and lower limbs are still covered with the scars of the wounds !

A bucket of tar was then brought, and two negroes were ordered to rub it upon his bleeding skin, and to cover him from head to waist. His hair and eye-brows were clotted with the tar. After this part of the ceremony was concluded, he was covered with feathers. His pantaloons were then drawn up to his waist, but he was not allowed to put on his shirt or coat. He was conducted, in this exposed condition

2 *

amid the shouts of the populace, to the railroad train, and was put on board the negroes' car. The engineer blew a continuous blast on his whistle to signalize the performance.

A citizen of Charleston on the train, who saw the poor fellow's unhappy condition, stepped into a neighboring hotel, before the starting of the cars, and brought a cup of coffee and some biscuits to relieve the sufferer's faintness. It was a timely gift, and gratefully received. But the Southern chivalry gathered around the Southern gentleman, and threatened him with summary vengeance if he repeated his generosity. The exasperated crowd detained the train, and called for more tar and feathers, for a further infliction upon their bleeding victim. More tar was brought, but more feathers could not be found; and after fresh tar was applied, cotton was stuck upon it instead!

When the train started for Charleston, the mob bade him good-bye, and told him that when he reached this city, he would receive 130 lashes! At every station between Columbia and Charleston, the engineer blew a prolonged whistle, and gathered a mob to add fresh insults to the wounded man. At length, on arriving, he was met by the police, conveyed to prison, and detained in his cell for an entire week. Here he received, for the first time, soap and water to wash off the tar, and oil to soften his sores. A mob several times threatened to break into the prison to carry him out into the street, and make a public spectacle of him a second time. But he was kept closely confined. A physician called to see him, to examine his wounds, who told him that his case was a mild one, comparing it with that of a man who was then lying in the City Hospital from the effects of 500 lashes, which had almost put an end to his life!

On Saturday morning last, at seven o'clock, the poor workman was taken from prison, and conducted quietly on board the steamer for New York. He arrived in this city on Monday last, where he is still staying, recovering from the effects of his ill-treatment, and looking for work, which we hope he may find.

We have only one comment to make on this case. This man informed us that, in common with the great mass of Irishmen in this country, he had always voted with the Democratic party. He had long known in Philadelphia that the Democratic party upheld slavery, but he never learned, until he went to South Carolina, that slavery crushed the white laborer, and that the Democratic party, in upholding slavery, is therefore the enemy of Irishmen, who are a nation of laborers. In the Southern States, wo.. is looked upon as dishonorable, and workmen as degraded. This is what an Irish stone-cutter learned while cutting stone in South Carolina. We hope the lesson of his experience may reach the ears of his countrymen! — *New York Independent.*

AN IRISHMAN IMPRISONED AND BANISHED.

In the Augusta (Ga.) *Evening Dispatch* of the 29th ult. is the following editorial paragraph : —

"ARRESTED. A man named James Crangale, hailing from Columbia, S. C., was arrested by the police, last night, for giving vent to Abolition sentiments, while in a state of intoxication, and is now in durance."

A second edition of this story is published in the Charleston (S. C.) *Mercury* of Dec. 31st, two days later, and is as follows : —

"VIGILANCE. Passengers from Augusta report that an Abolitionist was tarred and feathered in that city on Friday. His name is represented to be James Crangale, recently from Columbia."

Mr. Crangale arrived in this city, from Charleston, on Saturday last, in the steamer Nashville. His story we have from his own lips, and we think it may be repeated to the edification of Mr. O'Conor's countrymen who believe slavery to be an excellent institution, and who vote the Democratic ticket, and for the information of those Union-saving gentlemen who have debts to collect on account, or under judgments, at the South.

Mr. James Crangale is by birth an Irishman, educated to the law, who emigrated to this country about two and a half years since. Being under the necessity of earning a livelihood, he made an engagement, soon after his arrival in this city, to go as clerk into the establishment of Messrs. Gray & Turley, Dry Goods Merchants of Savannah and Augusta. After a brief stay in the former place, in the employment of Messrs. Gray & Turley, he was sent by them to the establishment at Augusta, when they refused to retain him longer in their service. He returned to Savannah, where he soon obtained the place of Deputy Clerk to the Court of Ordinary of Chatham County, Ga. Since that time, he has lived quietly, unobtrusively and inoffensively, busy with the duties of his office, and in qualifying himself to be admitted to the bar. With the subject of slavery he never meddled, and never, in any way, expressed an opinion in regard to it.

Feeling, however, that he had been unjustly dealt with by Messrs. Gray & Turley, who had induced him to go to the South, and had then broken the engagement between them, without regard to the consequences that might ensue to him, a stranger and friendless in a strange land, he sued them for his salary under the contract. The suit was brought in a Justice's Court, and a decision given in his favor. Appeal was made by Messrs. Gray & Turley to the Superior Court, where the decision of the Court below was confirmed, and judgment granted against the defendants. This end, however, was not gained without some difficulty. Three lawyers successively threw up his case, after delaying it for several months, and he at length carried his suit through, and brought it to a successful issue, by acting as his own counsel. But even here was not an end to the legal obstacles in the way of justice. With the judgments in his hand, he went to one after another of the officers of the law in Savannah, but could find none who would execute the duties of their office against a well-known, influential and wealthy house, in behalf of a poor and friendless Irishman. He appealed to the Solicitor-General, Julian Hartridge, to lay the conduct of these delinquent officials before the Grand Jury, but it was only to meet with a refusal from that gentleman, on the ground that an indictment against them would also involve one against the attorneys for the defendants.

Hopeless of redress in Savannah, Mr. Crangale went to Augusta, trusting that in that place, where Messrs. Gray & Turley are holders of property, he should be able to find officers who would serve the judgment of the Court against them. On his arrival, he went to the United States Hotel, kept by Messrs. Dobey & Mosher, and took a room. In the course of the evening, he was waited upon by a man, calling himself John Neilly, who invited him out upon the sidewalk in front of the hotel, and there said to him that, understanding him to be an Abolitionist, he, Neilly, on behalf of the Vigilance Committee, directed him to leave town immediately. Mr. Crangale at once refused to act on this order. He was there, he said, for the purpose simply of collecting money due him on a judgment of the Superior Court, and for nothing else; and that if they could prove him to be an Abolitionist, they were welcome to hang him. He was permitted, then, to return to the bar-room of the hotel, where he presently related the summons that had been served upon him, and the conversation that ensued. Thereupon, James Hughes, the bar-keeper, came forward and stated that he knew that Crangale was an Abolitionist; that he had this information from Andrew Gray, who said that "Crangale was a damned Abolitionist and rascal, and ought to be put out of the way." Mr. Crangale again denied the allegation. He understood now, however, the source and meaning of the accusation, for Andrew Gray is a brother of the senior partner in the house of Gray & Turley.

About two o'clock that night, when asleep in bed, his room was broken into by three constables, named Everett, King and Ramsay, accompanied by about twenty of the Vigilance Committee, who arrested him. They dragged him out of bed, and, after taking from him his overcoat and valise, hurried him off to jail. The next day he was waited upon by another constable, one Ford, who demanded his keys, which he refused to give up. Ford assured him that if no Abolition documents were found in his possession, he would be discharged; but if the charge against him should be proved, he would be hung up at the prison gates by the Vigilance Committee. To persist in refusing to give up his keys, Ford assured him, would be considered as equivalent to a confession of guilt, and he should call the committee to execute speedy judgment. Under these threats, he had no alternative but to comply with the demand for the keys, and surrendered them. In the evening of that day, Mr. Olin, a Justice of the Peace, called upon him, and informed him that Mr. Foster Blodget, Jr., the

Mayor of Augusta, had filed an affidavit against him, which was sufficient to swear away ten lives, if he had so many. This formidable document, which Mr. Olin showed him, asserted that he, the Mayor, had been informed and believed that the errand of Crangale at the South was to stir up an insurrection among the slaves, and that he was doing so; that he had asserted that the slaves would be justified in rising against their masters; that the people of the North would be justified in putting arms into the hands of the slaves; that the people of Massachusetts were justified in aiding and arming the "niggers" at Harper's Ferry; and that he, the Mayor, was prepared to prove these assertions. Mr. Crangale met these charges with a flat denial. He assured Mr. Olin that the whole story was a falsehood, a fiction from beginning to end; that he had never held and had never uttered any such sentiments. Mr. Olin thereupon informed him that his trial would take place the next day, and advised him to send for and engage as his counsel Col. Cumming, a well-known lawyer, and one of the most respectable and influential citizens of Augusta. The advice was taken, and Col. Cumming applied to. He called that evening, and, after listening to Mr. Crangale's statement, to his honor be it said, consented to defend the case.

All this time, it should be remembered, the prisoner was held under no legal process, but, though confined in the City Prison, and visited by the officers of the law, was simply in the custody of the Vigilance Committee. The next morning, he was ordered into Court, and on his way thither was arrested at the suit of the State, on a charge of endeavoring to incite an insurrection among the slaves, and was arraigned before Justices Olin and Piquet. The statute of the State which provides the penalty of death for the crime with which the prisoner was charged was read, when Col. Cumming moved that the case be carried to the Superior Court, which would sit the latter part of January, and that the prisoner be remanded to take his trial at that time. He gave as his reasons for this motion, that the present trial was held, in fact, by the Vigilance Committee, who alone constituted the audience, and who would hang the accused then and there, if the slightest shadow of suspicion could attach to him. Mr. Crangale himself, however, arose and opposed this motion. Strong in his own innocence, he wished the trial to proceed, and did not fear the result. The witnesses were then called and examined. They were Charles M'Calla, John Neilly, Allen Davy, Thomas T. Fogarty, and James Hughes, the bar-keeper at the United States Hotel. Their evidence, however, was only hearsay. Not one of them knew any thing, of his own knowledge, of the prisoner; not one of them had ever heard him utter a single Abolition opinion, or any opinion whatever, upon the subject of slavery, and none of them knew any thing about him, good, bad or indifferent. The only evidence of any moment was that of Hughes, who testified, on a cross-examination, that Andrew Gray had pointed out the prisoner to him as an Abolitionist; and that of Neilly, who acknowledged that he had agreed and proposed that the prisoner should be hanged, without the formality of a trial, at the time of his arrest, upon the lamp-post opposite the United States Hotel. This admission passed even without rebuke from the Court. But the Court was more vigilant when Hughes admitted that Gray had pointed out the prisoner to him as an Abolitionist, and ruled out the evidence, on the ground that the trade of Augusta with the North would be injured should it become known that such was their method of dealing with creditors. After the witnesses had been examined, Col. Cumming addressed the Court, in a speech evidently so fearless as to have exercised a strong influence over the minds of the Court and audience, and marked by a degree of sound common sense hitherto unheard of under such circumstances. He denounced these Vigilance Committees as self-made tribunals, constituting themselves at once witnesses and judges, and as actuated by no higher motive than a determination to denounce all Northern men of property as Abolitionists, for the purpose of ruining them and dividing the spoils among themselves. The statute of Georgia, providing the penalty of death for inciting the slaves to insurrection, he said, on the other hand, though severe, was none too much so. It behooved the South to keep both its eyes and ears open to protect their property against incendiaries. But the innocent, he declared, should not be accused and subjected to persecution. Under the effect of this speech, and as no tittle of evidence could be produced against Mr. Crangale, the Court had but one course to pursue, and the prisoner was acquitted. He

was nevertheless condemned to pay the costs of prosecution,
the fees of the Vigilance Committee who had arrested him
without legal process, and the cost of the imprisonment which
he had been compelled to suffer, and was remanded to jail till
payment was made. On arriving at the hotel, his coat and
valise, which the committee had taken from him, were produced, but the pocket-book, containing nearly a hundred dollars, and which he had left in the coat-pocket, was not to be
found. Again he was taken to the Court, where he stated
the circumstances to Justice Olin. But that gentleman
refused to believe him. "I have," he said, to the prisoner,
"acquitted you simply for want of evidence; but I still believe you are an Abolitionist, a God d——d Abolitionist, and
you had better confess it. You are," he continued, "a fool,
a God d——d fool. Have not your friends told you so?
Do you not know it yourself?" He then ordered him to
open his valise, declaring that if any thing was found in it to
convict him, there were enough of the "boys" present to
string him up. The prisoner at first refused to obey this order. The valise and the keys, he said, had been out of his
possession for two days; he did not know what might have
been put in the valise, and he did not choose to take the
chance of being hanged on such a contingency. On the
threats being repeated, however, he consented to open the
valise, which fortunately had not been tampered with, and
where nothing was found but his clothing and some papers
relative to the debt which he had come to Augusta to collect.
Word was then sent to Col. Sneed, the President of the Vigilance Committee, of the inability of the prisoner to discharge
the bill of costs, and to demand its payment of him, as the
representative of the party making the arrest. Col. Sneed
refused. The Mayor was then sought for to make the same
demand of him as prosecutor, but he could not be found. It
seemed perfectly clear to the Justice that the bill had to be
paid by somebody, and, as those from whom it was rightfully
due could not be compelled to, he chose to act on the principle that possession is nine points of the law, and hold him responsible whom he had in his power. A new committal was
made out, and Mr. Crangale returned to jail till he could pay
the costs of his own false imprisonment. After suffering a
further confinement of thirty-three hours, and it being evident

that there was no relenting on the part of his persecutors, he wrote to Col. Cumming to thank him for his generous services, and to ask for another interview on his behalf. Soon after, Mr. Alfred Cumming, a son of Col. Cumming, appeared at the jail, paid the fees demanded, and the prisoner was released. Mr. Olin had advised him to be off the moment he was out of jail, as there were " boys enough about," he said, " to string him up." As he had every reason to believe in the soundness of this counsel, he left immediately, and arrived, as we have already stated, in this city on Saturday.

We subjoin a copy of the bill for the non-payment of which Mr. Crangale was detained in the Augusta jail thirty-three hours; and had not this sum been generously advanced by Col. Cumming, he would, no doubt, have been still in confinement, unless, indeed, the old cry of "*a la lanterne*" had been fulfilled in his case, in *this* modern Reign of Terror.

AUGUSTA, Ga., Dec. 31, 1859.

MR. JAMES CRANGALE,

To Richmond County Jail,		Dr.
For three days' board, of self, at 50c.,	$	1 50
Turnkey's Fee,		1 20
Committing, Marshal and Constable cost,		11 58
Jailer, R. C.,		1 25

Received Payment, $15 33

URIAH SLACK.

It will be observed that Mr. Crangale still owes Richmond County, Georgia, twenty cents, if he ever owed it any thing, as Mr. Uriah Slack made an error to that amount in adding up the items. It is all he has gained to carry to the credit of his account against Messrs. Gray & Turley. — *New York Tribune.*

———

The Charleston *Mercury* publishes a letter signed " A Merchant," in which the paper's New York correspondents are requested to give the names of the leading Abolition houses in New York and elsewhere. For one, the writer pledges himself not to purchase one dollar's worth of goods from such parties as shall be designated.

AN EXILE FROM ALABAMA.

Every day, fresh instances of banishment are occurring in all parts of the South. Northern men are coming away in armies — driven out of sixteen States, and made exiles in their own country. A purser on one of the Southern steamers which arrived a few days ago in this city said, " We are having crowds of passengers, for we are bringing home all the Abolitionists." The men who are driven away are not generally Abolitionists until they become so after their expulsion. A peaceable workman in South Carolina, who never has had a thought about slavery until a mob tars and feathers him, and sends him to New York, becomes very naturally a strong Abolitionist by the time he reaches Sandy Hook. In this way, South Carolina is now doing more to make genuine anti-slavery men than all the North together.

Since our last issue, we have been called upon at our office by a fresh exile, who was recently driven away, in a very elegant and polite style, from a very aristocratic circle of society in Alabama. The manner of the expulsion was so dainty and chivalrous, that we cannot forbear to relate the circumstances.

Dr. Meigs Case, an intelligent and educated gentleman, formerly of Otsego county, in this State, went to Salem, Alabama, in September last, to take charge of the Alabama Female College. This institution, which had formerly been prosperous, had for some years past been running down, under the inefficient management of Southern teachers. Dr. Case, on arriving at Salem, found himself welcomed by the most intelligent part of the community, who said to him, " We have to look to the North for teachers, for we never yet have found a Southern man who was not too lazy to teach a school ! " Dr. C. found that the old " field-school," or the " ten-hour " system, was in vogue in that town, as in many other parts of the State. According to this system, the scholars and teachers go to school at daylight, and stay all day in or around the school-buildings. Each scholar recites, not in a class with others, but by himself. After his lesson is over, he roams about the grounds and indulges himself in a pleasing variety of idle amusements. This constitutes, in Alabama, " a day's schooling."

Dr. C., after receiving assurances of aid from the chief citizens of the place, agreed to undertake the management of the institution. He immediately began making arrangements for the thorough reorganization of the establishment. His design was to begin the first term with the beginning of the New Year. To this end, he wrote to the North, and engaged the services of assistant teachers, ordered from Northern publishers the necessary school-books, and sent for other members of his family. But while the teachers, the books, and the family were just on the point of starting for the South, he was waited on by a "Committee on the safety of the Union," who politely informed him that public opinion, during the last few months, had undergone such remarkable changes, that it was now no longer expedient to permit the residence of a Northern man in a Southern community. The time had come, they said, when Southern men must be watchful of their institutions, and must rid themselves promptly of all persons whose influence was likely to be cast, in however faint a degree, against the system of slavery. Dr. C. had never made any expression of views on either side of the question; but the fact that he was a Northern man was a sufficient pretext for his banishment. The gentlemen who had given him the most cordial welcome to the place were now the most active in procuring his summary dismissal. They stated, with true chivalric politeness, that they regretted to compel him to leave, but apologized by adding that the state of the times demanded prompt expulsion. They concluded their interview by urging him to quit the place at once, intimating that they could not be responsible for his safety if he remained longer than twenty-four hours. A leading physician in the town, who had professed great friendship for Dr. Case, said to him, in parting, "If you had been introduced to our citizens by the Governor of the State, and were as stanch a Democrat as any in Alabama, you still could not be sustained amid the excitement that now pervades all classes of the community."

At this time, a bill was before the lower house of the Legislature, entailing a fine of $500 on any school commissioner who should give a certificate of qualification to any Northern man who had not resided ten years within the State, and who was, moreover, not an owner of slave property!

Dr. Case, perceiving that to attempt to carry out his projected enterprise would not only be useless but hazardous, determined to take the most prudent course, which was to leave the State within the required time. He is now in this city, where he is in negotiation with several institutions of learning from which he has had application since his return.

If Southern men shall succeed in banishing all Northern teachers, the next generation of the chivalry will scarcely know how to read and write. — *New York Independent.*

TRIBULATIONS OF CONNECTICUT BOOK-AGENTS.

Two young men of this State—James J. Miller, of Hartford, seventeen years old, (large of his age, and looking older,) and Emmons J. Coe, of Meriden—have just returned from North Carolina with a rather uncomfortable experience of the manner in which some of the people of that region observe the guarantees of the Constitution.

They went to Salisbury, Rowan county, about four weeks ago, as travelling agents for L. Stebbins, publisher, of this place, to sell two large and handsomely illustrated volumes, "The History of the North American Indians," and "The History of Christ and His Apostles." They took a room at the Mount Vernon House, and, after thoroughly canvassing Salisbury and the vicinity, they went to Gold Hill on Monday, Nov. 22, and returned on the evening of the 23d.

On their way back, in the evening, they met two men returning from court, who asked, "Do you know Old Brown, the insurrectionist?" "No." "Well, you look out, or you will be in jail pretty soon." They heard nothing more until Wednesday morning, when, as they were looking at a fire which broke out in the Methodist church, Coe heard the Mayor say to a man standing by: "Yes, that's the very man; he stops at the Mount Vernon House." "Are you speaking of me?" said Coe. "Yes." He handed them his card, and, with Miller, returned to the hotel, whither they were followed by the man to whom the Mayor spoke. In a short time, an officer with five patrolmen, carrying heavy canes, came to their door. Miller opened it, and politely asked them in. He also offered them his trunk, his keys, papers, books, letters, &c., and invited them to satisfy themselves as to his character and business. They chose to take the young men directly to the police court.

Arriving there, accompanied by a great crowd, a scene ensued supremely ludicrous to any bystander who could have dared to laugh. Three magistrates presided. The trunks were brought in, the leaves of the books turned over and over, and laid aside for more careful study. The crowd questioned a good deal, and then swore a great deal, and then questioned and swore more. They opened carefully and shook out every shirt and pair of trowsers, but no treason appeared.

The presiding magistrate said that there was nothing against them but suspicion, yet he thought it better to bind them over for trial before the Superior Court, requiring $500 bail! They asked Miller and Coe if they were ready to give bail? "Certainly not," said Miller; "take us to jail."

So they went to jail, with a solemn procession of six officers around them, and ten couples in front, and six more in the rear. They sent for a lawyer, R. B. Moore, who proved himself a frank, generous, sensible friend throughout. They had crowds of visitors daily asking to see the "d—d Yankees," or the "d—d Abolitionists."

On Tuesday, the 29th, they were brought into the Superior Court, and the prosecuting attorney told the Court that "these young men were ignorant of the laws, and, so far as ascertained, had committed no intentional offence," &c. The judge lectured them, for what nobody knew, and told them that on paying their jail fees, $4.12 each, they should be discharged. They paid the bill, but returned to the jail for protection from the mob of "lewd fellows of the baser sort," who manifested great anxiety to use tar and feathers.

In the evening, the sheriff escorted them to the hotel, where they kept close. Crowds gathered at the depot, hoping to get a chance at them as they took the cars. On Wednesday evening, November 30, gatherings in the street indicated a disposition to mob them, and they armed themselves, with a determination to resist, and the landlord told them, "If they tar and feather you, they shall tar and feather me also." On Thursday at noon, they quietly took a buggy for Lexington, a station some miles distant, where they waited, appearing not to know each other, for the night train. Excepting some close questioning at Portsmouth, they met no further difficulty, and took the steamer for New York.

Among the ridiculous and wholly baseless stories against them, it was said that they had called slaves into gin shops, talked two hours with them privately, sold them books, and told them that if they would only run away somewhere "across the river," the invading army that came to rescue Brown would take them off, and also promised to correspond with, &c. &c. They heard threats in abundance daily, but escaped without serious loss, aside from the breaking up of their business and the expenses of their defence.

We trust that the outrages of which this is but one sample out of hundreds will receive a decided rebuke on Wednesday evening from our "Union-savers."—*Hartford Press, Dec.* 12.

A NEW-YORKER EXPELLED FROM KNOXVILLE.

On Monday, a man from New York, by the name of Cregar, was taken up by a committee, who waited on him, and brought him before a meeting of our citizens in the courthouse, upon the charge of being an Abolitionist. He was called upon to state his own case, and he did so by saying that he had been forced to leave Asheville upon a short notice; that he was an anti-slavery man; had rode in a wagon with a slave near Asheville, and had told the negro what wages were at the North, &c. According to his own version, he is an Abolitionist; but he said that he had not tampered with any slaves—did not believe it right to run negroes out of the South, and he was opposed to getting up insurrections. His business was to sell fruit trees and shrubbery for an extensive establishment at Rochester. The excitement was very great, the crowd was large, and at one time, the consequences threatened to be serious. Rev. James Park opened the meeting with a sensible address, in which he counselled moderation, and expressed the hope that the citizens would preserve their dignity, and calmly listen to reason, and not to the suggestions of passion. We considered his remarks well-timed, and his sentiments proper, and we stated to the meeting that we endorsed the sentiments of Mr. Park, and urged upon the citizens to act in keeping with their magnanimity of character, and not to inflict personal violence upon the man, unless they had other and stronger testimony against him. At this stage of the game, the sentiment of the crowd was that Cregar ought to be required to leave the State in a reasonable length of time, but that he ought not to be treated with violence. But Gen. Ramsay, the lately defeated candidate for Congress, came down upon the stand, and delivered one of the most uncalled-for, ill-timed, not to say infamous, speeches we ever listened to under the circumstances. He was for crucifying the man, as an example to others. He was grossly insulting to all who counselled moderation; he made the political party issue, and placed all who were not for violence in the attitude of hostility to the South, and launched out against the Union and in favor of dissolution.

Col. O. P. Temple followed Gen. Ramsay, and gave him a most severe, but merited, castigation for the speech he had delivered, denouncing his sentiments as worthy alone of scorn and contempt, and was loudly cheered by the audience.

Speeches were also made by James R. Cooke, Esq., and Will L. Scott, Esq., who took the proper view of the subject, and counselled moderation, deprecating the great evil of mob law prevailing to a dangerous extent in the South, and hoped that reason, moderation and justice would be acted out on this occasion.

After these speeches were delivered, the committee of three, who were out, brought in a report requiring Cregar to leave in twenty-four hours. This was, as we understood it, so amended as to allow him three days to wind up his business, and this, we are inclined to think, met with the approval of the meeting. But an unfortunate debate sprang up between Messrs. Park and Charlton, and the consequences threatened, for a time, to be fearful, as the friends of these gentlemen drew weapons. But, by the interference of friends, peace was restored, the crowd dispersed, and the New-Yorker has left for his congenial North, where he ought to remain. — *Knoxville (Tenn.) Whig.*

———

TAR AND COTTON.

A case of applying these two commodities to the epidermis of an individual was practised in this city, Thursday night, under the following circumstances : Sewall H. Fisk, a dealer in boots and shoes, on Market square, of several years' standing, has been the object of suspicion for some time, in consequence of his known abolition proclivities, which he has taken, as we are informed, some trouble to make known to our slave population. His latest acts are, enticing negroes into his cellar at night, and reading them all sorts of abolition documents, and last Sunday night was devoted especially to the history of the trial of John Brown, and a general exhortation upon the institution of slavery and the advantages of freedom. These facts, as we hear, were sworn to before a Justice of the Peace by his nephew and his clerk; and coming to the ears of some parties who have constituted themselves a quasi-vigilance committee, Mr. Fisk's store, over or in which he sleeps, was visited, and he was called out and gagged before he could make either noise or resistance. He was then placed in a carriage, and driven a short distance from the city, and the application, as above, made to his nude person; he was then left to find his way back as best he could. His first appearance in the limits was near the hospital, where he came in sight of a watchman, who was so alarmed at the sight, that he gave a spasmodic jerk at his rattle, and took to his heels, not willing to face so dreadful an apparition. A reinforcement, however, was brave enough to approach him, when he was conducted home, the most pitiable object it is possible to imagine. Not a spot of his skin was visible, and his hair was trimmed close to his head. — *Savannah (Ga.) Republican, Dec. 3d.*

A BOUNTY ON KIDNAPPING.

In the Maryland Legislature, in January last, Mr. JACOBS, of Worcester, offered the following :—

"Whereas, at the 24th anniversary of the American Abolition Society, held in the City Assembly Rooms, in New York city, in May, 1857, a certain Francis Jackson, of Boston, Treasurer of the Society, reported that during the current year the receipts of the Society were $19,200, and of the auxiliary societies of New York, Pennsylvania and Michigan, $18,856; making a total of $38,162 from those sources; and,

"Whereas, said American Abolition Society also received for the same year, as appears from said report, the further sum of $158,750 from the Exeter Hall Emancipation Society, in the city of London, Great Britain, and both of said two sums make an aggregate of $196,912; and,

"Whereas, the London *Times*, a newspaper of high repute on all questions involving the policy of England towards this country, distinctly declares that this money was given as a bounty on slaves—i. e., to decoy them from their owners, and induce them to run away; and,

"Whereas, a certain Hiram K. Wilson, of Worcester, in Massachusetts, did go into Canada, and take a census of all such runaway slaves during the winter of 1856, and reported their number at 35,000, since augmented to 45,000; and,

"Whereas, a certain Thomas Garrett, of the city of Wilmington, in the State of Delaware, did attend the anniversary meetings as aforesaid in the city of New York, in May, 1857, and did there show by his books of record and entry, where he had stolen 2,059 slaves, and forwarded them North, per underground railroad; and,

"Whereas, said Garrett did attend a meeting of Abolitionists held at the Assembly Buildings, in the city of Philadelphia, on the 17th December, 1859, whereat he stated, that by his books of entry and record, he had stolen and conveyed North by the underground railroad the further number of 386 slaves, since the report in May, 1857, making a total of 2,445 slaves stolen by said Garrett; and,

"Whereas, the said sum of $196,912, bestowed upon said Garrett in May, 1857, and his large annual receipts per capita for every slave he can so steal, have made him rich in wealth, and marked him as a wicked and base traitor to man and God; and,

"Whereas, most of the slaves so stolen by said Garrett belong to citizens of this State, whose rights of property the State is sacredly pledged to secure inviolate—therefore, be it

"Resolved, by the General Assembly of Maryland, That the Treasurer pay, upon the order of the Comptroller, the sum of ——— to any person or persons who may secure said Thomas Garrett in some one of the public jails in this State; and that the Governor of this State, on information of such fact, is hereby requested to employ the best legal ability of the State to prosecute said Garrett to conviction and punishment."

Mr. JACOBS then entered into a detailed explanation of the resolution; of the manner in which slaves are stolen from Worcester and other counties in that vicinity. He dwelt at

3

some length upon peddlers, their tricks of trade, and the insinuating way they have of ingratiating themselves into the good-will of negroes. He was particularly hard on Garrett; said he was a traitor, and should be hung.

About having slaves run of, Mr. Jacobs had experienced loss from that cause. He now had a man in Canada who often wrote home begging for money and to be brought back. The poor devil was nearly starved, but could not come back, although he wanted to do so. Mr. Jacobs verily believed he was run off by "Old Brown." Garrett, who sent his minions, the peddlers, throughout the country, pocketed the money for running them off. Mr. Jacobs denounced Garrett as an arch-traitor, a villain, and guilty of every horrid crime. There were men that he knew who could convict the scoundrel, and he wanted him caught. As a matter of course, under the rules of the House, the resolutions of Mr. Jacobs lie over for another reading.

Subsequently, Mr. Jacobs asked a suspension of the rules, so as to call up his resolutions providing for the capture of Thomas Garrett, for running off slaves from Maryland. The rules were suspended.

Mr. Jacobs moved that the blank in his resolutions for the capture of Garrett be filled with $2,000.

Mr. McCleary moved to amend with $500.

Mr. Chaplain moved to amend the amendment by $5,000.

Mr. Gordon thought it best first to change the resolution of Mr. Jacobs, so that the bounty would not be paid until Garrett was convicted.

Mr. Dennis asked, if this man was in the State, what could be done with him?

Mr. Jacobs. Hang him. (Laughter.)

Mr. Dennis resumed. According to the gentleman's statement yesterday, Garrett was never in Maryland. If a citizen of another State receives slaves from Maryland, and forwards them to Canada or elsewhere, he cannot be touched for violating the soil of Maryland. The thing is out of the question.

Mr. Gordon, of Allegany, said that without an examination of the questions, he was not prepared to coincide with the gentleman from Somerset. If a man stands on the Virginia bank of the Potomac, and shoots another in Maryland with a rifle, is he not amenable to the Maryland laws? Certainly.

If by means of emissaries, he, on the borders of another State, steals a horse, and runs him off, is he not just as amenable to the laws of the State which he violates in that manner? And so it was with negroes.

Mr. DENNIS, of Somerset, replied that there was no analogy in the cases. In the one instance, there is a direct violation of the soil of the State; in the other, it is asserted that a man in another State has gotten rich from the per capita of slaves run off, as the resolutions say, from this State. Allowing that it could be proved that they were run off from Maryland, he could not be harmed. He had never been in the State. We do not know that he had emissaries, and if he had, it is a question not for decision by this House.

Mr. GORDON rejoined. He said it was admitted that Garrett sent emissaries into the State; that he had publicly boasted of having, through their instrumentality, run off slaves from Maryland. That gave the question another aspect, and it should be well considered.

Mr. JACOBS said he had no doubt but that Thomas Garrett could be convicted, if taken. He cited several instances in which the fact that he ran off slaves could be proved.

Mr. DENNIS asked why Mr. Jacobs or some other gentleman had not gone before the Grand Jury and had him presented, if these statements were so notorious.

Mr. JACOBS spoke warmly; denounced the London *Times* and the New York *Courier*, and declared that before he would have Maryland become secondary to the North, he would go in for a dissolution of the Union.

Mr. LONG, of Somerset, moved to refer to Committee on Judiciary.

Mr. JACOBS. Will that kill it, or not? (Laughter.)

Mr. LONG. The resolutions embrace important considerations, and should be referred to the Committee. They were the creatures of the House, and their action, therefore, could either be adopted or not by the body creating them.

Mr. JACOBS. You are Chairman of that Committee, ain't you? (Laughter.)

Mr. LONG. No, sir. I am, however, on the Committee. Mr. Gordon is Chairman.

Mr. JACOBS. Ah, well, I will trust it to him. (Laughter.)

After some debate as to the propriety of referring the matter, Mr. Jacobs consented to the reference. The whole matter—resolutions and amendments—was then referred. (1)

(1) In a letter from this widely known and greatly esteemed Quaker philanthropist, published in a Delaware paper, with reference to the malicious and absurd things charged against him by Jacobs, in the Maryland Legislature, friend Garrett says:—

"In order to disabuse the public mind, I will state a few facts to show that the charges made by said Jacobs are false. I am charged with having acknowledged that I had stolen over two thousand slaves from their masters, at so much per head, which, with the large receipts from Great Britain and other sources, amounted to the handsome sum of one hundred and ninety-six thousand nine hundred and twelve dollars, which had made me rich in wealth, and marked me as a wicked and base traitor to God and man. If there was any truth in the above statement, I ought to be rich, at any rate. I will now give the facts respecting the above statement, and those who know me, I feel confident, will put implicit confidence in what I say: those who do not know me may doubt my veracity; that I cannot help, and shall give myself no concern about it. As to the stealing of slaves, I utterly deny the charge. I never, since I came to the State of Delaware, thirty-seven years ago, asked or persuaded a slave to leave his master or mistress, neither have I, in a single instance, sent a peddler, or any other human being, to persuade, entice, or bring away a slave, much as I detest slavery; but I have made it an invariable rule, if called on for advice or assistance by a slave, or any one in distress, to render such assistance and give such advice as I thought they needed. This I have never denied. And if I found a slaveholder in distress, needing assistance, I would endeavor to aid him; but should be very apt to let him know, before we parted, that I looked upon slaveholding as the venerable John Wesley did, as the sum of all villanies.

"I will now state what I solemnly affirm to be true, that I have expended in clothing and in different ways, for the comfort and assistance of colored people, voluntarily, several thousand dollars, and that I have never received from Great Britain, and all other sources together, one thousand dollars, to assist God's poor.

"In addition to the above sum, which I have at different times expended, some years since, I took a family of colored people out of Newcastle jail, by habeas corpus, before Judge Booth, Chief Justice of Delaware, who, in consequence of the commitment being defective, released them all. The parents admitted their two eldest children were slaves, but assured the judge, sheriff, attorney, and myself, that the father, mother and four

THE REIGN OF TERROR IN VIRGINIA.

To the Editor of the New York Tribune:

SIR: As I observe that your statements as to the risk of travelling at the South are doubted by your neighbors of the *Times* and *Herald*, permit me to relate a fact in my own experience of very recent occurrence.

younger children were free. It was raining at the time; the family wished to go to Wilmington; a hack was hired, at my suggestion, to take the mother and four small children to Wilmington. I forbade the hackman to take the father and two eldest boys. He insisted on taking them all with one Horse, and I told him, before he left, if he took the father and two sons, he must look to them for pay, as I would only pay the price agreed upon for taking the mother and small children; and to this day, I have never paid him more than the price agreed upon. One of them was eight months, the other three years old,—a cripple with white swelling, that could not walk a step. Suit was brought against me, first under the law of 1793, where the fine was $500 each for aiding a slave; and then, after being fined by Judge Taney, before whom I was tried, $3,500, suit was brought by the slaveholder's attorney, James A. Bayard, for the value of the slaves; and the agent of the mistress of the mother and four young children was called on by Judge Taney to fix the value on the whole lot, and the jury awarded, as their value, $1,900 more, making $5,400 fine in all. I think he admitted that the mistress of the woman had offered to sell her time to her husband, several years before, for $100, but said she was worth $300 to sell to the traders. If I am not wrong in my recollection, he also stated that the mistress lived nearly twenty miles from the family, that the father had maintained the four young children from their birth, and that the mother had not lived with her mistress for about ten years; but he stated the mistress always intended to claim the children after they were old enough to become valuable. There was no charge of crime against me but the hiring a conveyance to bring them from Newcastle to Wilmington. I was tried for aiding the two eldest while I was sick in bed, in consequence of which my attorney declined defending me, and of course I was convicted, and fined $500 each, when I had no more to do with violating the law than Judge Taney himself, or James A. Bayard, the prosecuting attorney.

"From the above statement of facts, the public may see how much truth there is in the statement of my friend Jacobs, that I had become rich by the aiding of slaves to escape.

"THOMAS GARRETT."

For fifteen years past I have been in the habit of visiting the South, having certain interests in Tennessee which require my personal attention. In the latter part of January, I was on my way to Tennessee, with Judge Platt, of Yonkers, and Mr. Lewis Edwards, of Orient, L. I. When passing through Virginia, I fell into conversation, somewhere between Lynchburg and Bristol, with a fellow passenger. After some talk upon indifferent matters, this person asked me "if New York merchants did not feel the withdrawal of Southern trade." I replied that it was too early in the season as yet to judge whether there had been any diminution of trade from such a cause. "I am," he continued, "interested in two mercantile firms, and I have given orders to both that they shall purchase no goods north of Baltimore, and not even there, except of direct importation." "You have," I answered, "a perfect constitutional right to buy your goods where you please. We are, however, glad to deal with you as long as you pay your notes. The South," I remarked further, on some allusion on his part to Northern sympathy for John Brown, "does not understand the feeling of the North in regard to that affair. Not a hundred people among us knew of Brown's intention, or approved of his acts when known, however much they might admire the character of the man. And on that point," I added, "no one has paid him a higher compliment than Gov. Wise, who said he was the pluckiest man he ever saw."

"Sir," said my interrogator, with a good deal of emphasis, "before having any further conversation with you, I wish to know what you think of Helper's book."

"I have never read it," I replied.

"At any rate," said he, "you cannot be ignorant of its contents. But I will tell you what it advises: it advises non-slaveholders to cease all intercourse with slaveholders; not to employ them either as physicians or lawyers, not to trade with them, nor to go to communion with them. *Now,* what do you think of it?"

"Have you ever read that work yourself?" I asked.

"I have not," said he.

"Then," said I, "I think that you are not the proper person to interrogate me upon this work, nor am I the proper person to criticise it, when we have neither of us read it."

But this did not satisfy him. He wanted and insisted upon having a more positive answer. At length I said: "I acknowledge that Virginia has a perfect constitutional right to continue or to abolish slavery as she shall see fit, and that we of the North have nothing to do with it. This should satisfy you as to my opinions of the Helper book."

But this was not enough. He wanted a more positive expression of opinion on the book itself.

"It seems to me," said I, "that the question is one that belongs to you alone. It is simply a quarrel among cousins. The book was written by the South, in the South, and for the South, and we commercial men at the North care very little about the matter any way."

He burst out here with great violence and vehemence: "Sir, I believe you are a d——d Yankee Abolitionist! I am a member of the Vigilance Committee, and I will have you arrested and examined!"

"I am," I answered, "a merchant of New York, passing through the State on my way further South, where I have large interests, and am on my lawful business."

He continued his abuse, reiterating, "You are a d——d Abolitionist! I will have you arrested and examined!"

Presently he asked me for my address, which I gave him without hesitation. "I," said he, "am Fayette McMullen. I have been for eight years a member of Congress from this State, and two years the Governor of Washington Territory. And you," he repeated, "are a d——d Yankee Abolitionist, and no gentleman." Here I turned my back upon him and took up a newspaper. Then he left me; but going through the car, he pointed me out to a number of persons as an Abolitionist. My fellow passengers were some of them Southern men, and some Northern. With many of these passengers I had travelled from Washington, and we had been together for four and twenty hours. It was to this circumstance, perhaps, that I owed it that Mr. McMullen's attempt to get up an excitement against me was a failure. There were some muttered remarks, it is true, undoubtedly intended for me, such as "that any Abolitionist going through the South ought to be tarred and feathered;" but I was not molested. My assailant went through the other cars of the train, with the amiable intention, I presume, of having me mobbed. He failed, however, there also, and finally returned to his seat near me, and went to sleep after his labors.

NEW YORK, Feb. 23, 1860.   J. C. HAZELTON.

A GERMAN CITIZEN HANGED, BEATEN AND ROBBED.

Yesterday, (says the Quincy (Illinois) *Whig*, of February 25th,) a respectable German citizen of LaGrange, Missouri, Mr. Frederick Schaller, (a brother-in-law of Mr. H. Dasbach, of this city,) who has resided in LaGrange for the last twelve years, was brought to Quincy a victim to the horrors of a pro-slavery outrage, the recital of which is enough to make the blood of any man, who has a soul, boil in his veins.   We called upon Mr. Schaller and obtained the statement which we publish below.   We saw the bloody evidence of the horrible treatment he had undergone, heard the story of the affair as given by him, and could not help believing every word of his statement.   He is a respectable and intelligent man, and his plain and simple account of the dastardly outrage, was, we venture to say, implicitly credited by the hundreds of our citizens who called at Mr. Dasbach's yesterday.

Mr. Shaller has always voted the Democratic ticket, and we are assured by German citizens of Quincy, that in his visits to this city, he has defended the institution as it existed in Missouri.   That he is innocent of the charge of assisting negroes to escape — as he asserts — we have no doubt.

We trust that our German citizens, especially those who have been in the habit of voting the Democratic ticket, will ponder well this flagitious outrage, and then determine whether they can continue to vote with a party whose cardinal principle is the spread and extension of that institution which is the parent of such damnable and brutal lawlessness.

We are under obligations to the editors of the *Tribune* for the translation of Mr. Schaller's statement : —

STATEMENT OF MR. SCHALLER.

I have been a resident of Missouri for twelve years, having resided a part of the time in Palmyra and part of the time in LaGrange.   In the latter place I have property.   I have never meddled with slaves or slavery, and have always been a Democrat.

Late last fall or early in the winter, I heard that ten slaves had run off; I knew nothing about it till I heard of it, and do not recollect of ever having seen them. I could therefore not have aided their escape. Nobody in LaGrange ever suspected me of tampering with slaves, till last Sunday. I went on that day to Canton, to invite some friends to a party that was to take place last Tuesday. On my arrival there, I was waited upon by three persons, Jim Ring, Josh. Owens and Bill Webster, who informed me of my being under suspicion of having aided the escape of a slave of Mr. —— Harris, and that I would have to return with them. At first I took the matter for a joke, but soon found that they were in earnest. On the night on which the slave ran off, who was caught again, at *ten* o'clock, I can prove by twelve or fourteen persons that I was in my house till twelve o'clock, consequently could not have aided the negro.

I returned with the three, satisfied of my innocence, and asked for a fair trial only, as I easily could have proven my innocence. I was taken to the LaGrange House, and asked to be tried next day, (Monday,) but was refused. Monday night an armed posse of twenty-five or thirty men came, tied our (my brother William's, Nob. Mattis's, who had been taken before my return from Canton) and my hands, and put us into a hack. Two others, Frank Gerlach and a Mr. Holmes, were set free, but ordered to leave town. Our hands were tied, and we were driven in the hack about three miles on the Memphis road, where the hack stopped, and I was taken out. To my question where they were taking me to, I got the answer that I was to be hanged. I asked them what for, and received as an answer, that I should tell them all about the nigger scrapes, about Vandoorn, etc.

As I knew nothing about them, had never seen or heard of Mr. Vandoorn, I could not give the answer they wanted. They took me about a quarter of a mile into the woods and hanged me. I caught the tree, but, by beating my hands with sticks, they compelled me to let go my hold. Soon I was senseless. When I came to again, I felt two persons, one on each side, whipping me with whips or cowhides. My hands were tied to the tree above my head, and I was entirely naked. The night was very cold, and soon my back was covered with a crust of frozen blood. I became weaker, and when they untied me, I fell to the ground. I heard one of them say,

3*

" Now you can go, you son of a bitch ! "   When I put on my
clothes again, I found my money ($128 in gold) and watch
gone.   As I could not stand, I crawled, as well as possible, to
the house of my father-in-law, where Dr. Niemeyer treated
me.

My brother, whom they had released, told me that they
must have abused me for more than an hour.

I again say that I am as innocent of the charge as a child,
and have never aided the escape of slaves.

The American (Mattis) is still in LaGrange, sick from a
similar treatment.

FREDERIC SCHALLER.

———

BANISHMENT OF A SCHOOL-MISTRESS.   Within the last few
days, an occurrence took place in one of the young ladies'
schools of this city, which shows that even Yankee school-
teachers, who come South to make money, cannot keep a dis-
creet tongue in their head.   Abolition is in them, and it will
gush out one way or another.

In the case in point, some of the young lady scholars were
talking over the excitement of Harper's Ferry, and one or
more of them expressed an opinion, saying, " Old Brown
ought to be hanged ! "   The teacher from down East, who,
we understand, gave lessons in music and French, rebuked the
young pupils for calling the Kansas murderer and robber
" Old Brown," and stated that they should name him as " Mr.
Brown," that he was engaged in a meritorious cause, and was
a good and brave man, whose object was not evil, &c.

The young daughters of the South did not relish this lauda-
tion of the old sin-dyed rascal, who would incite, pay and arm
negroes to maltreat or murder them ; they made known the
expressions of the Yankee teacher to the Principal of the
Academy, who, after investigating the matter, immediately
discharged the offending teacher.   She made tracks for the
North the same evening, but will, doubtless, make capital out
of the occurrence somewhere down in Maine or Massachusetts,
where every feminine, who is just able to spell " c-a-t," thinks
she can teach all Southern children. — *Richmond Enquirer.*

A HIRED TRAITOR IN OUR MIDST—PASS HIM ROUND.

Our attention has just been called to a copy of the Clarke *Journal*, (a weekly sheet, published at Berryville, Clarke Co., Va.,) bearing date the 11th inst. This journal is professedly Democratic in politics, and now keeps the following ticket at the head of its leading columns:—

For President — R. M. T. HUNTER, of Va.

For Vice President — D. S. DICKINSON, of N. Y.

Under color of this show of conservatism, the editor of the paper, Alexander Parkins by name, publishes *as an advertisement* the full prospectus of the New York *Tribune*, occupying an entire column, and for which, doubtless, Mr. Parkins receives a considerable moneyed compensation. That our readers may properly appreciate the nature of the inflammatory article thus *paid for and published within a few miles of Harper's Ferry*, we reproduce the following sample of Greeley's prospectus:—

"The 'irrepressible conflict' between Darkness and Light, Inertia and Progress, Slavery and Freedom, moves steadily onward. Isolated acts of folly and madness may for the moment give a seeming advantage to Wrong; but God still reigns, and the Ages are true to Humanity and Right. The year 1860 must witness a memorable conflict between these irreconcilable antagonists. The question, 'Shall Human Slavery be further strengthened and diffused by the power and under the flag of the Federal Union?' is now to receive a momentous, if not a conclusive answer. 'Land for the Landless versus Negroes for the Negroless,' is the battle-cry of the embodied millions, who, having just swept Pennsylvania, Ohio and the North-West, appear in the new Congress, backed by nearly every free State, to demand a recognition of every man's right to cultivate and improve a modicum of the earth's surface, wherever he has not been anticipated by the State's cession to another. Free Homes, and the consecration of the virgin soil of the Territories to Free Labor — two requirements, but one policy — must largely absorb the attention of our Congress through the ensuing session, as of the People in the succeeding Presidential canvass; and, whatever the immediate issue, we cannot doubt that the ultimate verdict will be in accord at once with the dictate of impartial Philanthropy and the inalienable rights of man."

We merely suggest to the good people of Jefferson and Clarke counties that the squad of Yankee peddlers lately ordered away from their borders are emissaries of a much less dangerous description than that to which Mr. Alexander Par-

kins belongs.   A hired disseminator of Abolition treason is
the very man of all others to tamper with slaves, to run them
off, or, if he had the courage to do so, to lead the van of servile insurrection.   Whether Mr. Parkins has not already laid
himself liable to fine and imprisonment in the county jail for
his complicity with Horace Greeley's incendiary efforts, is a
question which we recommend to the careful consideration of
the prosecuting attorney of Clarke county.   But there can be
no doubt whatever that the people of Clarke and the sur-
rounding counties owe it to their own safety to suppress this
incendiary sheet.   A respectful request to Mr. Parkins to
leave the community, signed by all his subscribers, would perhaps prove efficacious; but don't lynch him.   The friends and
supporters of Messrs. Hunter and *Dickinson* should especially
attend to this matter.   The impudence with which Parkins
attempts to shelter his treason behind the names of these
worthy gentlemen deserves especial reprobation. — *Richmond
(Va.) Enquirer, Nov. 15th.*

FREE SPEECH IN VIRGINIA.

Every body in Virginia knows or ought to know that she
has a set of laws for the especial government of her negro
population, bond and free, one of which makes it an indicta-
ble offence, punishable by fine and imprisonment, to give utterance to Abolition language and sentiments.   We know that in
the so-called free States this interdict is severely commented
upon; but if they will persist in sending their emissaries
among us to corrupt our negroes and entice them away from
their owners, they deserve themselves whatever odium may be
attached to such a law, the necessity for enacting which they
have enforced upon us.   All we ask of strangers coming
among us from those States is implicit obedience to our laws,
be they good or evil in their eye; if they are not prepared to
yield it, let them pack up and quit our borders; otherwise
they are to expect no immunity for their disobedience.   The
thing is very simple, and cannot possibly be misunderstood,
we should think, even by a crazy Abolitionist.   Yet instances

of a disregard of this provision of our municipal code are by
no means unfrequent; and two have occurred here since that
of S. Danneberg, which we mentioned a few days ago. One
was that of a clerk in a store, a young Scotchman, who strongly
advocated the conduct of Old Barabbas Brown. His employer,
having more compassion for him than Old Barabbas had for
the wives, mothers and children of Virginia, gave him his discharge without subjecting him to an arrest, and, following the
advice of a friend, he "took out in the first boat" for the
North.

The other was that of a resident on Ferry Point, opposite
this city, John Fletcher by name, who came from Washington
City some five years ago. On Tuesday last, in the grocery
store of his neighbor, Mr. James P. Jones, in the presence of
ten creditable witnesses, while in conversation about the Harper's Ferry affair, "he avowed himself an Abolitionist, and
asserted that there were many in Norfolk and Portsmouth,
but that they were afraid to say so; but he was free, white
and twenty-one, and had no hesitation in declaring that if he
had five thousand dollars, he would give one-half of it for the
release or rescue of John Brown."

The bystanders were highly indignant at such language,
and immediately had information of it lodged with T. Port-
lock, Esq., J. P., who thereupon issued his warrant for the
apprehension of Fletcher. The warrant was given to officer
John M. Drury to execute, who proceeded to Fletcher's dwel-
ling, and knocked for admittance at the front door; but he
made his appearance at a side door, and, being told by the
officer that he must go with him, said he would do so, and retired to get his coat and hat; but on his return, said he had
changed his mind, and was determined not to be taken. The
officer then attempted to seize him, when he held the door
nearly closed with one hand, while with the other he drew a
knife, which he held up in a threatening manner, and said,
" d———n you, if you attempt to enter, I will kill you." Mr.
Drury then went and summoned persons to his assistance;
and on his return, Fletcher, after consulting with members of
his family, and being threatened with a forcible entrance by
the posse without, quietly surrendered and was taken off to
jail, to undergo an examination. — *Norfolk (Va.) Herald.*

DASTARDLY OUTRAGES UPON NORTHERN CIT-
IZENS AT THE SOUTH.

WASHINGTON, D. C., Nov. 28th, 1859.

Slavery has taken another advancing step, and this time it
is free speech which has been stricken down in the capital of
the country. I allude to the case of Dr. Breed, referred to
in my last letter. The main facts, agreed to by all parties,
are as follows : A gentleman who has lived in peace and respectability in Washington for the last seven years — who has
had high office under successive administrations — a Quaker
— calls upon a neighbor upon business. He there meets a
stranger, and is introduced to him. The two gentlemen talk
of John Brown — get excited — both say extravagant things
— get cool afterward — make up — shake hands, and part.
The next day, one of the parties is arrested for the expression
of his sentiments respecting slavery, and he is forced to take
his choice of a prison, or give $2000 bonds to keep the peace
for a twelvemonth ! No man swore that he was afraid Dr.
Breed would attack him ; not only that, but the man (one
Dr. Camp) who instigated the arrest of Dr. Breed, himself
threatened the life of Dr. Breed if he *dared* to utter certain
sentiments respecting slavery.

Your correspondent attended the trial before Justice Down,
and is forced to say that it was a farce from beginning to end.
The two witnesses covered each other's tracks in their testimony ; one of them swore positively that he did not believe
either of the gentlemen (Van Camp and Breed) knew what
they said — that they were much excited — and that he did
not suppose Dr. Breed meant what it is alleged he said. It
was evident to every body present that it was simply an angry
private discussion between two persons who call themselves
gentlemen. Dr. Breed utterly denied, before Justice Down,
the utterance of the sentiments imputed to him ; and none of
his friends here, who know him to be a Non-Resistant on principle, for a moment credited the statement of Van Camp.
Justice Down seemed to have no idea of law or justice, for
he bound Dr. Breed to keep the peace in the sum of $2000,
on the ground that, if he had uttered his sentiments before

slaves, or a white audience, it would have endangered the peace of the community! What an insolent defiance of all law and justice!

In the court-room, a gang of ruffians was gathered, and threats were openly and loudly made to take the life of Dr. Breed on the spot. One man cried out in open Court: "Let's hang him up when he goes out!" and no man reprimanded the scoundrel for his offence. The *Star* very candidly admits that if the police had not been present in strong numbers, Dr. Breed would have been in danger. This affair did not occur in Virginia or Naples, but in the capital of the United States! Henceforth, Washington is to be set down as a spot where freedom of speech is not allowed. Any member of Congress may be thrown into prison by this so-called Justice Down, for words uttered in private conversation, and left there till he will give bonds.

Brooks was fined three hundred dollars for making a murderous assault upon a United States Senator in his Senatorial seat; while a Northern man is held to bail in the sum of two thousand dollars, and but for the presence of a friend, would have gone to jail, upon a charge of using "seditious language." He might have blasphemed God, or threatened to dissolve the Union, with impunity; to speak against slavery is the unpardonable sin. — *Correspondence of the N. Y. Evening Post.*

A NINE YEARS' RESIDENT DRIVEN AWAY FROM ALABAMA.

We have authentic information, that a gentleman who has resided for nine years in Georgia and Alabama was driven away from home a few days ago, and forced to take a hurried passage to the North, leaving behind him his wife and children, and a thriving business, which must now go to wreck. What was his crime? He had not only never spoken against slavery, but always in favor of it. He honestly held Southern sentiments, and was always ready to avow the same, although he could never persuade himself to own a slave.

His profession was that of a teacher of vocal and instrumental music.

A fortnight ago, a book agent was arrested in a town in Alabama for soliciting subscribers to "Fleetwood's Life of Christ," published by a Northern publisher. The Methodist Conference was in session at that time, and the case was noticed on the floor of that body. The members advocated the unfortunate agent's immediate expulsion from the place, on the ground that his continued presence would be dangerous to the existence of Southern institutions! A paper was drawn up, adopted, and published in the newspapers, setting forth the ground of their action, substantially as follows:—

"We have examined this man's case. We find no evidence to convict him of tampering with slaves, but as he is from the North, and engaged in selling a book published at the North, we have a right to suspect him of being an Abolitionist, and we therefore recommend, in order to guard ourselves against possible danger, that he be immediately conducted by the military out of this county into the next adjoining."

Accordingly, the militia were called out, and the poor book-peddler was summoned to receive military honors. But this was not all. The musician of whom we have spoken, a nine years' resident, whom nobody ever suspected of being an Abolitionist, was called upon to ride at the head of the procession, *and play the flute!* He immediately declined, and took occasion to express his opinion that the agent had done nothing worthy of his expulsion. The procession accordingly marched without the flute player. In the evening, greatly to his surprise, he received an anonymous letter (whose source, however, he could not fail to detect) commanding him, under penalty of tar and feathers, to leave the State immediately. He knew the people too well not to be wise enough to take the hint. His wife, who was a Southern lady, and had never been in the North, was thrown into great grief on reading the letter, but advised her husband to leave before daylight, as she feared for his safety if he remained longer. So at three o'clock in the morning he saddled his horse, and taking with him what clothes he could put in his saddle-bags, galloped away—an exile from home and friends! He has since reached a Northern city, and is now making arrangements to bring his family to a place where they can breathe freer air.— *N. Y. Independent.*

MOB VIOLENCE IN KENTUCKY.

LETTER FROM WM. S. BAILEY, EDITOR OF THE "FREE SOUTH."

The many reports thrown into circulation since the ungallant attacks made upon me and my principal office by certain individuals in our city, have moved many of my friends, and the friends of common justice, to inquire into the cause of such an unlawful procedure.

The cause, so far as made known to me on Friday night, October 25th, when they carried off the inside forms and destroyed them, was, that they wanted a charter for a bank in Newport, and that the Legislature would not grant them one while my paper was printed here. But it is hardly likely that the Kentucky Legislature will grant a bank charter to a party of house-breakers and sackers, to strengthen them in such fearful acts of violence.

Not a word was spoken to me on the subject until the first night of attack—the combination being a dead secret, unknown to me or any of my friends.

The next day, (Saturday, 29th,) no excuse was offered, but a demand made to enter my office again, to carry off the remainder of my printing material. I expostulated with them; told them it would be an injury to their own standing as men, a disgrace to the city of Newport, and no credit to the cause espoused, viz.: slavery. But all the pleadings of myself and family were in vain. They procured a heavy plank, and battered in the door with the end of it, entered, and took out all they could get out, and left the house a perfect wreck.

The heart-rending sorrow of my family, working so many years, night and day, so long as our physical strength would allow, and being harassed by the law for debt, (after the destruction of my former office and machine shop by incendiarism,) sued for slander because I published the truth upon a man who had acted unjustly in his official capacity as sheriff—wading through all these trials and troubles of six years duration, and beginning to live a little more comfortable, mobocratic violence has fallen upon us again, and our whole means of subsistence been destroyed. To stand by and behold these ravages filled the hearts of my family with irrepressible grief.

It is well known by the citizens of Newport that I have been among the foremost in the encouragement of all our public improvements, and have spent much time and money to that end.   *   *   *   *   *

The stories told about me as having correspondence with Brown at Harper's Ferry, and the officers there having a letter from me to him, are without foundation or truth. I never saw Mr. Brown—never wrote to or received a line from him in my life, nor knew any thing about his movements until the difficulty was published in the newspapers.

Falsehoods have been thrown into circulation here by persons professing the most frantic terror at the "horrible" thing I was about to do; that I contemplated the capture of the United States Barracks of this place, intending to arm the negroes here (although there are none to arm) and commence war upon the slaveholders in the State; but how any person could be so credulous as to believe such an extravagant story is alone with the wicked plotters who destroyed my office to conceive.   *   *   *   *

On the first night of attack, a pocket-book, containing *one hundred and fifty dollars*, which I handed to my wife, was lost in the confusion, and has not been heard of since.

My loss in printing material and damage to the house is about *three thousand dollars*.

I have transgressed no law of Kentucky, nor do I intend to do so; but I ask protection from lawless violence in the legitimate publication of my paper. I dislike the taking up of arms, even in self-defence; but, for the righteousness of my cause, the dignity of my State, and the honor of my people, I shall maintain my position, and labor, and I ask the friends of true American liberty to aid me. The spirit of freedom and true greatness is beginning to be planted upon Kentucky soil, and it illy becomes the legal authorities to stand aloof and suffer the freedom of speech and of the press to be trampled under foot, to stifle that liberty which tyrants in all ages have sought to overthrow.

WM. SHREVE BAILEY.

Note. The Grand Jury of Campbell county found bills against about a score of persons for a riot, in the destruction of Mr. Bailey's paper, the *Free South.* The State's Attorney, hearing of this, argued the matter before them, taking the ground that it was the law that where a nuisance existed which could not be reached by law, the people had a right to abate it. The jury sought the opinion of Judge Moor on the question, and he told them that it was the law; whereupon they reconsidered and quashed the indictments!

VIRGINIA RUNNING OUT WHITE MEN.

Some years since, Mr. Reuben Salisbury, then of Sandy Creek, in this county, and brother of Mason Salisbury, Esq., disposed of his property, and, with his family, removed to Virginia, where he engaged in the business of farming, and where he led a peaceable and peaceful life, until the unfortunate occurrence at Harper's Ferry. He was a quiet man, a member of the Baptist Church, and estimable in all the relations of life. Though not an advocate of, nor an apologist for, the institution of slavery, he was a man who attended to his own business, meddling with nobody's slaves, and questioning no man's privilege to hold them, if he was satisfied that it was right to do so. He was a man of rare integrity and moral worth, charitable, tolerant—in short, a good man.

Well, a short time since, a complaint was lodged against this gentleman, who is now about sixty years of age, some kind of a process obtained, and about twenty of Virginia's chivalric sons deputed to execute it. They were all armed, and, visiting the premises in a body, they had no serious difficulty in capturing Mr. Salisbury. A search was then instituted for evidence to sustain the charge that had been preferred against him. His house was ransacked from cellar to garret; every nook and cranny was peered into, and his private papers fumbled over, and the hunt had well-nigh proved fruitless, when a few copies of the *Albany Evening Journal*, which had been sent him by his friends in Sandy Creek, were discovered, and the venerable old man was hurried off to jail. Here he remained several days, but was finally admitted to bail, and by the advice of friends, was induced to quit his home in the Old Dominion and the State of his adoption. He returned to Sandy Creek last week. His farm in Virginia he advertises for sale at auction, and expects it will go at a sacrifice of from $2,000 to $3,000.

So much for Virginia justice. We ought to add, that the magistrate before whom Mr. Salisbury was arraigned belonged to the same church with that gentleman, for that will show the kind of Christianity they have down in that section.

This occurrence has created considerable sensation and no little indignation among Mr. Salisbury's former neighbors and

friends. And is it remarkable that it should? Turning to
the Constitution of the United States, and learning that the
object of that instrument, according to the preamble, was to
"establish justice" and "secure the blessings of liberty," they
very naturally ask themselves if "liberty" and "justice" have
not, in this instance, been ruthlessly trodden under foot?
John Brown and four others were adjudged guilty of murder,
and have been executed, for their attempts to *run black men
out of Virginia;* what is the offence of those other men who
are engaged in running *white men* out of the State? If it be
a high crime to seek to deprive slaveholders of their property,
is it a justifiable proceeding to divest non-slaveholders of
theirs? Are doings of this sort calculated to increase our
respect for the Union, to allay the anti-slavery feeling at the
North, and bring us over to the faith of those who are opposing what they term "sectionalism"? Has the time indeed
come when people living South must stop reading Northern
newspapers? Shall we of the free States be denied the privilege of sending papers to our friends who have gone South
to reside? Shall we stop corresponding with them, lest we
get them into difficulty?

We cannot reconcile these things with our notions of justice. If a man leaves New York and takes up his residence
in Virginia, we expect he will conform to the laws of the
latter State, and in so doing he ought to be protected in his
person and property, and we think he would be, if the head
of the Government cared as much for the rights of freemen
as for the wishes of the slaveholding oligarchy; in other
words, if our Federal Executive was an impartial ruler.
Such a ruler may we not hope to elect in 1860?—*Pulaski
(N. Y.) Democrat, Dec.* 29.

————

A mob of pro-slavery men recently broke up a school
taught by Robert Milliken, at Kirksville, Mo. He was con-
ceded to be a good teacher, and personally unobjectionable,
but was guilty of having a father who had incautiously expressed anti-slavery sentiments in a letter to a friend in New
York!

A SHAKER CITIZEN OF COLUMBIA COUNTY EXPELLED FROM VIRGINIA.

Among the many ludicrous incidents consequent upon the raid of the eccentric and fanatical man, the late John Brown, upon the unsuspecting and peaceable citizens of Harper's Ferry, there was one in which a resident of this county bore a very conspicuous part.

One of the peaceable and exemplary Shakers from New Lebanon, in this county, was on his yearly tour through south-western Pennsylvania and the adjacent parts of Virginia, peddling his garden seeds, or rather, supplying his old customers with their usual stock for the ensuing spring demand. While quietly moving along the highway with his horses and wagon, with a close box (painted green, probably) in which his seeds were packed, secure from rain and fogs, and without even knowing that he had passed the boundaries of Pennsylvania, and entered into the land of chivalry, he was suddenly arrested in his progress, and charged with being an incendiary Abolitionist. His vigilant captors were informed that though his closed wagon-box contained materials that would *expand*, if properly sowed in their gardens in the spring, they were not really of an *explosive* nature.

The Virginia vigilants were incredulous, strongly suspected that he was a very dangerous character, and proceeded with due care and caution (probably fearing that some "infernal machines" were mixed up with the small boxes containing seeds) to overhaul and examine the contents of the wagon. Though finding neither powder, nor Sharp's rifles, nor warlike pikes, they were far from being satisfied that all was right—pronounced him to be a very suspicious and dangerous character, and lodged him in jail, or some other safe "lock-up," for the night.

On the following morning, a company of brave and chivalrous militia was assembled, with muskets and bayonets in hand, and, with the soul-inspiring music of fife and drum, he was safely escorted and guarded back from "Old Virginia's shore" into the State of Pennsylvania, and the agitation and alarm caused by his presence in that part of the "Old Dominion" quieted and allayed; and then did the chivalry breathe calmly and freely again.

This incident is regarded as eminently worthy of being recorded in history as the first occasion on which it was found necessary to call out a military company for the protection of the citizens of any community from the evil designs of an unoffending, unwarlike and non-combatant Shaker.—*Kinderhook Rough Notes.*

LYNCH LAW MEETING IN SOUTH CAROLINA.

A public meeting (says the Kingstree (S. C.) *Star*) of a portion of the citizens of Williamsburg District, S. C., was held at Boggy Swamp, at Mr. McClary's store, on Tuesday, the 22d inst., for the purpose of taking the preliminary steps of ridding the community of two Northern Abolitionists, who have been for some time teaching school in said district. The two characters are W. J. Dodd and R. A. P. Hamilton.

Nothing definite is known of their Abolition or insurrectionary sentiments, but being from the North, and therefore necessarily imbued with doctrines hostile to our institutions, their presence in this section has been obnoxious, and, at any rate, very suspicious; therefore the meeting was called. On motion, Samuel W. Maurice was called to the chair, and James Potter acted as Secretary. On taking the chair, the Chairman explained the object of the meeting, whereupon, on motion, it was

Resolved, That, in the opinion of this meeting, the presence of W. J. Dodd and R. A. P. Hamilton in this community, under the present critical condition of public affairs, touching the institution of slavery, is obnoxious; and although we entertain great respect for the persons in whose employment they have been, yet we deem their longer continuance here as being so dangerous and suspicious as to be our sufficient apology for taking some coersive measures for their removal.

Resolved, That a committee of twelve be appointed to proceed forthwith to the whereabouts of said Dodd and Hamilton, and give them notice that they will have until Saturday, the 26th, to leave the District.

The chair appointed the following as a Committee to wait upon them :

R. C. Logan, *Chairman;* T. S. Chandler, Dr. W. L. Wallace, John M. McClary, T. A. McCrea, W. H. Griggs, R. H. Shaw, James Potter, S. J. Strong, Wm. McCullough, Enoch Dudley, James C. Murphy.

Resolved, That another public meeting of all citizens in the District favorable to the move is hereby called in the court-house at Kingstree, on Saturday, the 26th, M., to hear the report of said Committee; and if said gentlemen do not quietly leave, pursuant to notice, by that time, that then such measures of a coercive character will be adopted as in the opinion of said meeting may be necessary to put them off by force.

Resolved, That these proceedings be published in the Kingstree *Star.*

On motion, the meeting adjourned, and the Committee proceeded to the performance of their duty instanter.

S. W. MAURICE, *Chairman.*

JAMES POTTER, *Secretary.*

———

PUBLIC MEETING.

At a public meeting (says the Sumter (S. C.) *Watchman*) of the citizens assembled on Wednesday afternoon last, at the Town Hall, Col. G. S. C. DeSchamps was called to the chair, and T. W. Dinkins, Esq., requested to act as Secretary. The Chairman having stated the object of the meeting, asked if gentlemen had prepared business for the consideration of the meeting; whereupon the Chair (in conformity with a motion to that effect) appointed the following Committee to report on business: T. W. Dinkins, D. J. Winn, H. L. Darr, A. Anderson and W. L. Pelot. The Committee, in a few minutes, reported the following preamble and resolution. After discussion, they were unanimously adopted : —

Whereas, disclosures of an inflammatory character are brought to our notice by every mail, showing that it is time for every slaveholding community to be on the alert for its own security and protection of its interests; and whereas, notwithstanding the warnings from the press growing out of the present state of the country, stragglers from the North continue to visit and tarry in our town as agents for books, medicines, &c., whose real object may be to act as spies and Abolition emissaries; therefore,

Resolved, That we, the citizens of Sumter, in public meeting assembled, do call upon and request our Town Council to institute a rigid surveillance on all such transient persons; and where full satisfaction is not given, to notify such persons that their presence in our community is not to be tolerated.

It was further moved and adopted, that a committee of five be appointed to lay the foregoing preamble and resolution before the Town Council.   In accordance with which motion, the Chair appointed Messrs. W. E. Dick, L. P. Loring, H. Haynesworth, A. A. Nettles and Dr. J. L. Haynesworth a committee.

It was also resolved, that the meeting, when adjourned, be adjourned to meet again on Wednesday next, 23d inst., at 11 o'clock, and that an invitation be extended to the citizens of the District to attend and co-operate in measures for the public safety.

G. S. C. DeSCHAMPS, Chairman.

T. W. DINKINS, Secretary.

VIRGINIA INDIGNATION.

A large meeting of the citizens of Barbour and adjoining counties was held at the Court House in Phillippi, Virginia, on the 7th ult., the same being court day for said county, to express a public sentiment concerning the late insurrection at Harper's Ferry.   Among the resolutions passed were the following : —

" Whereas, we contemplate with shame and detestation the late deadly affray at Harper's Ferry, from which it appears that a treasonable scheme has been for some time in preparation by certain instigators and emissaries of '*Irrepressible Conflict*,' '*Higher Law*,' and Abolition doctrines, whose end and aim is an assault and warfare upon the constitutional and guaranteed rights of the Southern States of our great confederacy; and whereas, by this attack on an arsenal of the United States, in the heart of the nation, and on the soil of our beloved Virginia, encouraged by advices and counsels from individuals in various of the Northern States, and emboldened by the appliances of money, and stores of arms and ammunition, furnished by accessories to this treacherous scheme of plunder and murder, it is evidenced to our belief that no mere riot of deluded fanatics was intended, but that a great, bloody and destructive project of *civil war* was contemplated, in which our servants and citizens, in co-operation with their Northern leaders and abettors of this rebellion, were expected to join in the plunder and butchery of their masters and brothers; therefore,

" Resolved, That we will, at all times, as Virginians and citizens of the United States, hold ourselves ready, as one man, to bear arms, even to death, if necessary, in defence of our constitutional rights, our liberties, and our homes.

" Resolved, That while we deprecate this invasion of Harper's Ferry as the ebullition of a blind and misguided fanaticism, which has resulted in bloodshed and the loss of the lives of valuable citizens of our State and country, we, notwithstanding, assert a confidence in the conservative element and spirit of the mass of the Northern people, and that our brethren there will unite with us in strengthening the bonds of government, the preservation of law and order, and in suppressing the incendiary movements and purposes of an infuriated and misguided portion of their population, who blindly plot the destruction of the Union.

" Resolved, That a committee of thirteen be appointed, whose duty it shall be to notify all persons in our county, known to be Abolitionists, to leave the county of Barbour in sixty days, if there should be any in our county."

Six Salesmen Sent Back to New York. A large and well-known business house in New York (who carry on a large trade with the South in the two articles of liquors and Union-saving) were greatly surprised to find that their great zeal in getting up the recent Union meeting had profited them nothing among their Southern customers. Six of their salesmen and agents were summarily forced to leave the South, and recently returned to their employers. Perhaps the firm will think twice before they sign a call for another meeting at the Academy of Music.

4

The New York *Journal of Commerce* says that the following incendiary handbill was received, a few days since, "by a highly respectable citizen, an American by birth, a patriot and a Christian, to whom it was addressed through the post-office. The envelope was post-marked Montgomery, Alabama, Nov. 25. The carrier who delivered it remarked to our informant that he had several others of the same appearance, addressed to other persons in his beat. It is probable that a large number of the same have been forwarded to different places at the North and West."

[CONFIDENTIAL.]

TO THE IRISH FRIENDS OF THE SOUTH IN THE NORTHERN CITIES.

FELLOW-CITIZENS,—You who have always been true to the Constitution and the South—who have never degraded yourselves to the level of the African race, as the dirty Free-Soilers do—you are aware that the borders of Virginia have been profaned by the tread of the Free-Soil assassin. The South looks to its Irish friends in the large free cities to effect a diversion in its favor, and for this purpose the United Constitutional Irish Association has been formed, of which some of you are (and doubtless all will be) members. In the great cities, prominent Free-Soilers and Abolitionists own large factories, stores and granaries, in which vast sums (made out of the South) are invested. This fact furnishes a means of checking their aggressions on the South; and the Irish friends of the South are relied on to make the check effective. Property is proverbially timid. Whenever a hay-stack or cotton-gin is burned at the South by Free-Soil emissaries, let a large factory, or a plethoric store, or an immense granary, in New York or Boston, be given to the flames. To make this course safe, your Association must be true to itself and its principles; method, caution, your double secrecy, will insure the safety of the actors. Southern gentlemen will be constantly among you, amply supplied with means to remove those whose patriotism has subjected them to suspicion. Besides, many friends will be found, both among Southern steamers' crews, railway conductors, and the police. In fact, you will find friends and funds on every hand. Be energetic, therefore; go at once to your *Foreman*, and see if he cannot introduce you to the Association, if you are not already a member.

Let us urge you to disseminate among your fellow-laborers the idea that you have not wages proportioned to the present high scale of prices. When once the mass of your country-men are filled with the notion that the Free-Soil capitalists are withholding the price of Irish labor, while trying to incite the negro of the South to rebellion, it will be easy enough to gather large mobs of your brethren, and when large mobs assemble, ware-houses may be burst open or fired. Be careful, however, that only the property of Abolitionists is harmed; every where protect those who are friendly to the South and true to the Constitution.

Irishmen! the South relies on you! Depend on it, that for every dollar's worth of injury to our enemies in the Northern factories, &c. &c., by riot or the torch, the South will amply compensate, and, besides, furnish you a safe refuge and a homestead. ☞ Remember to apply at once to *your Foreman, for particular instructions.* If he should not be able (which is not likely) to inform you, show this privately to some Irish gentleman of intelligence, after ascertaining his feelings towards the South. Thousands of copies of this con-fidential circular will be sent by Irish people in the South to their friends at the North.

THE COMMITTEE.

November 23, 1859.

———

SHOCKING CASE.

Glastenbury, Conn., Dec. 28th, 1859.

The Rev. Mr. Alberton was brought to his home — three miles from here — last Friday, with one leg broken and his head and arm bruised, by a fall from the cars, on his way home from Alabama, where he went a few weeks since, in the employ of Mr. Stebbins, of Hartford, peddling books. He was arrested after the John Brown invasion, on suspicion of evil designs, and imprisoned twelve days. The suspicion was

founded on a passage found in a letter to another person, in
the same business, from Mr. Stebbins. The suspicious sentence was this: "Take the best men, be faithful, do your
work thoroughly; my agent in this section is the Rev. Mr.
Alberton, whose head quarters is at ————." I don't recollect the name of the place. On this expression they founded
a suspicion of treason, and sent forthwith to the place and
arrested Mr. A., and the mob gathered around and cried out,
"Shoot him, shoot him!" "hang him, hang him!" He was
searched, tried, and false charges were brought against him,
and he was thrust into prison. He was so excited that he
finally had turns of derangement.

His case being reported to Mr. Stebbins, he procured the
testimony of persons in Hartford, Gov. Seymour and others, who
could be trusted, and he was released, and paid $60 for false
imprisonment. He was put on board of a steamer on the Alabama river to Montgomery, and thence by cars came home.
ᵀn a fit of derangement, he jumped out of the cars this side
of New Haven, and lay from 6, P. M., Thursday, to 8,
A. M., Friday, when he was found, and accompanied to Hartford.

I saw him on Monday of this week. He is very feeble,
and lies prostrate, bruised and mangled, like the "man who
went from Jerusalem to Jericho, and fell among thieves."
He is unable to talk much yet, he is so exhausted and excited.
He has a family consisting of a wife and six children; is an
Englishman by birth; has preached in this part of the town
five years, and has preached in this country about ten years.
He owns a house in Manchester, and suspends preaching on
account of the inconvenience of moving about with a family
of small children. He is a whole-souled, large-hearted Englishman and Christian; a man of unblemished moral character, and in good standing. He spent last winter in North
Carolina, and preached at times on the Sabbath to his own
and all other denominations.

Yours, &c.,   F. SNOW.

———

Helper, the author of the *Impending Crisis*, had a lot of
his books burned at Maysville, Ky., a short time since.

THE LYNCH CODE ENFORCED.

Correspondence of the Newbern (N. C.) Daily Progress.

SALISBURY, N. C., Nov. 20, 1859.

A few days ago, two Abolitionists of the most flagrant
kind, from Connecticut, under the guise of book agents, were
put in jail here. At their examination before Mayor Shaver,
many damning facts were elicited in connection with their
prowlings through Salisbury and neighborhood, in the
shape of tampering variously with slaves, pulse-feeling of
non-slaveholding whites, confabing with free negroes, &c.;
indeed, they were arrested in a free negro house, in which it
was stated they had sojourned, *a la Hotel de Dumas!* All
this, together with the incoherent and contradictory statements made by themselves, relative to their business and
movements, warranted the Mayor in ordering them to jail to
await a trial. The indignation of the citizens was so wrought
up that the miscreants begged piteously for protection, from
the office to the jail.

On Saturday forenoon, an Irishman, named Tait, was loudly announcing to a crowd in front of the post-office that he
was an Abolitionist, and that he hoped before long every
slaveholder's throat would be cut; he has been in this vicinity some eight years, and, by those who know him, is said to
possess a fine *school* education — to have been a bookkeeper
at one time here. Since I have been here, two years, he has
been a common laborer, very low in his conduct and associations, and habitually drunken; he is also said to be very
quarrelsome, very cowardly, and, covertly, very malicious,
spiteful and revengeful. I mention these facts that you may
understand the rather culpable leniency of the people here in
this case. Well! continuing to express his worse than seditious sentiments and wishes, a crowd soon gathered, by whom
he was seized and carried down to the yard of the Mansion
Hotel, where, I really believe, had he retracted, they would
have let him go, in consideration of his having been in their
midst and known to them so long (an aggravation of his crime,
in my mind); but when questioned, he repeated what he had
before said in a mocking and spiteful manner; also acknowl-

edged to and glorified in having wrote passes for the slaves
of Mr. J. Clark (one of his examiners) and others, to trade
with, &c.   They then proceeded to remove a luxuriant crop
of dirty red hair from his head, after which they *peeled* him
to the waist.   The day being rather cold, and it being resolved
to ride him out, "without horse, saddle or bridle," they humanely replaced the articles of covering of which they had
divested him with a very neat-fitting garment of North Carolina manufacture—tar is the name; but this was not enough,
for the more fastidious and tasteful J. B., who, resolving to
combine the ornamental with the useful, rushed into my neighbor C.'s room, seized one of his pillows, and soon had its contents all artistically attached to Tait's new coat; it was a
complete success; and I remarked to some one that, with
their limited practice, they could "tar and feather" with
neatness and dispatch.   Now, to a man of mind, principle
and honor, such a degradation would be worse than death, and
he would die rather than submit to it, but of such men Abolitionists are not composed, particularly those who have been
living any length of time in the South, where they have am-
ple opportunity to know the negro and his position; their
sentiments are caused by that malignant and jealous hatred
and envy which is too often found to exist in the hearts of the
ignorant and vicious poor towards the good, the intellectual
or the wealthy, or to all combined.   When they rode Tait
out, he did every thing like a buffoon, to attract attention;
this disgusted me so much that I did not follow.   I thought
that his thus glorifying in his disgrace as well as his crime
would incense the parties who were carrying him out of town
to such an uncontrollable degree that they would hang him,
and he richly deserved it, for the necessities of the times im-
peratively demand terrible examples, through short trials and
condign punishments, in such cases.   They only ducked him
two or three times in a creek, however, and let him go, he refusing to leave the State or retract any thing he had said, and,
when at a safe distance, turned and threatened several of the
parties with a speedy and terrible vengeance.   A crowd of us
went down to see the upshot of the affair, and finding him
gone, and learning particulars, blamed them for their forbearance in thus letting him go, worse than he was before.   Some
then started after him on horseback.   It was twenty-four

hours before they recaught him. He is now in jail, with the two precious villains from Connecticut. All irresponsible (*i. e.*, non-property holding) parties from the North, at the present time, are naturally enough looked on with distrust by the people here, and all of them who have deeply pondered on the subject of slavery, and are still anti-conservative, should immediately leave. The peace of society here and their own personal safety require it; for the criminal suggestions of the higher law delirium, which they attribute to inspiration in their unprincipled leaders, will be viewed here as something worse than the oozing out of distempered natures and the vapors of spleen, which are the mildest terms possible by which to designate their diabolical rhodomontade.

COSMO.

NEW-YORKERS EXPELLED FROM SOUTH CARO-LINA.

To the Editor of the New York Times:

I see in your *Times* of Monday last, I am put down as one of the unfortunate individuals lately sent away from South Carolina with a "new coat of tar and feathers." Not quite so bad as that, but, nevertheless, I was sent away, and without the least shadow of a reason. I had gone down there like any other honest Northerner, with trunk and books, and recommendations, and, having got a place in a little village by the name of Orangeburg, went to teaching. Thinking myself perfectly secure, and having got a very good place, I began to be considerably satisfied, when suddenly my quiet was broken up, and I was ordered to take my books and recommendations and trunk, and start for the North. It was a week ago on Saturday last, about two o'clock in the afternoon. I thought it best not to confine myself too much to my room, but take a walk. Accordingly, I took a short tour of the village, stopped at the post-office, and then called on one of my friends. To avoid suspicion of being thought an insurrectionist or an emissary of John Brown, as the Southerners think all the Northerners among them are, I had been especially careful not to say or do any thing that would at all alarm, not even whispering that slavery was an abominable thing, nor attending any of their "nigger meetings," except once or twice by special request, and in company with some of my friends.

Such being the case, one would naturally think himself safe enough in any place, especially in one that professes to have reasonable men. So I thought, but, having stayed awhile at my friend's, and read his papers, I was on my way back to my boarding-house, thinking, I believe, about Coleridge — something or other of his speculations — "Stop a minute, if you please ; going up to your room ?" and before me were standing Capt. Salley, Maj. Glover, and one or two others I did not know. Meaning to pass the time of day, and not expecting any such visitors, I was unprepared for receiving company ; nevertheless, I gladly accompanied them to my room, and, as politely as I could, gave them seats. "Hem ! We might as well commence business," said Capt. Salley. The rest assented, and then he went on to say that they had been appointed a committee, by the citizens of Orangeburg, to inform me that I must leave the place in the next train. If he had said, Take a trip in the New York City across the Atlantic, I could not have been more astonished. "You surprise me," I said, and wanted to know the reason of such a course. This was the contemptible thing offered as such : "They had come to the conclusion I was not exactly a proper person to be allowed among them, on account of my political sentiments." How they knew my political sentiments was, of course, a mystery ; for no one there knew them. But they chose not to reason further ; "the exigencies of the times demanded it." I "might be innocent for aught they knew ; but the case was such, the innocent had to suffer with the guilty." I asked them for a chance to vindicate myself ; I asked them for time to collect my bills ; I asked them to lend me money to get away with. They granted neither. I then appealed to them as men endowed with reason ; showed the cruelty and foolishness of what they were doing ; but the only answer to every thing was : "You must expect *the consequences*, or leave town by the next train," which would be in about two hours. They did, however, at last agree to collect my bills, and give me money enough to get to Charleston; and having assured me I should not be troubled by a mob, left the room.

I left it, too, a short time afterwards, considering it best to go where my own will might control the ways and means of my own body — this flesh and bones that troubled them so, because it came from the far North. I thought it best to take care of it, and not let it get broken, or bruised, or covered over with Southern slime, mixed up with prickly quills. This is the sum and substance of the affair, though I might say a good deal more of other men who were sent out in the same way, and some, alas! who got the " tar and feathers." I do not blame all the Southerners. A good many I found whole-hearted, noble souls, whose memory I shall always cherish; but those men who sent me away, and the brainless hotheads, generally, there, I hardly know what to think of. I would have said nothing about them — not wishing myself to be connected with their little, silly, villanous affair — but they have already put it in the papers; and it is only justice to myself and friends prompts me to give as much as I have, *merely a plain statement of facts.*

THREATS OF EXPULSION.

Resolutions of a public meeting at Beaver Dam Depot, composed of citizens of Hanover, Louisa, Spotsylvania and Carolina Counties, Va.: —

1. Resolved, That all classes in our community have one common interest in opposing the wicked intermeddling of the Abolitionists in our affairs.

2. Resolved, That we pledge ourselves to each other to keep a strict eye on all suspicious persons, particularly on all strangers whose business is not known to be harmless, or any one whatever who may express sentiments of sympathy or toleration with Abolitionists, either directly or indirectly.

3. Resolved, That Vigilance Committees, twenty-five in number, be appointed to act in the 4th and 6th magisterial

4 *

districts, whose especial duty it shall be to carry out the foregoing resolutions, in which all our citizens are expected to co-
operate; all suspected persons are to be brought before the
chairman of each committee, who, with any two members,
may act, and either bring them to trial or drive them from
the neighborhood, as may be determined.

4. Resolved, That the Delegate and Senator from this
county be requested to endeavor to have the law of criminal
trials so amended that a Justice of the Peace may be authorized to require the Sheriff in this county to empanel a jury
for the trial of any person brought before him on a charge of
encouraging or promoting insurrection or insubordination
among the slaves; and also to have the sentence of the jury
executed without delay.

EXPERIENCE OF AN INDIANIAN IN KENTUCKY.

Cove Spring, Mercer Co., Dec. 20th, 1859.

Mr. B. R. Sulgrove:

Dear Sir,—I will endeavor to write you a few lines, and I
know it will surprise you and my friends. I started from
Indianapolis last Monday, the 14th. Little did I think, when
I got here, that I would be notified to leave the State, or take
a coat of tar and feathers for being an Abolitionist. On
Saturday, I went up to Harrodsburg from here; and when I
came back, there was a company of slaveholders here to arrest me for being a negro-stealer from the North, and they
notified me to leave the State. I told them I was ignorant of
the laws of Kentucky, but I thought the law of the land was
that before they could hang a man, they must find him guilty,
and therefore I should not go until I got ready.; and if they
chose to apply the tar and feathers, they could pitch in; but
I thought they would have a warm time of it before they got
through. That is what they call Democracy here — the man
that can scare and catch the most men from the North here

is the man they intend to run for the next Congress. But I told them I did not come from Indiana here to be run off by a pack of ruffians. I told them I lived in a free State, and was a Republican; that every man spoke his sentiments there, and, thank God, I was glad of it. They may hang me yet — I can't say what they will do — but I want it distinctly understood that I am no negro-lover.

I was going to start back to-morrow, but I shall remain longer, to let them know that they can't scare me: and if any thing worse occurs, I will try and let you know.

Yours,

WM. S. DEMOTT.

—

Since the above letter was put in type, we have seen Mr. Demott himself, who has returned home. He says he was arrested on Monday following the writing of his letter, and put in jail till the next day, when he was released on $500 bail. The charge against him was that he was tampering with some body's slave. He was on a visit to some of his relatives, and his guilt has just the extent, and no more, of being an Indianian. His attorneys, Hon. J. F. Bell, the Opposition candidate for Governor last fall, and Mr. Fox, certify that there was no evidence of the truth of the charge. The fact is that the feeling in Kentucky, as in all the other slave States, makes criminal purposes of the mere presence of free State men; and while this feeling lasts, it is actually useless for an Indianian to visit the interior of Kentucky, unless he chooses to play the lick-spittle to their prejudices. The arrest of Mr. Demott, from all that we can learn, was nothing, and was intended to be nothing, but the most offensive mode of insulting and outraging his Republican opinions. He made no concealment of them, though he did not offensively parade them, and his imprisonment shows the appreciation that Kentuckians have of freedom of speech and opinion. People from that State will never be molested here for an expression of their opinions. May be they may learn some time that it will be wisest for them to show equal liberality. — *Indianapolis Journal, Dec. 24th.*

GROSS OUTRAGE.

The Belfast (Me.) *Age* publishes a letter from a correspondent in Georgia, giving the revolting particulars of a
gross outrage committed upon a ship's crew near Jefferson-
town, in that State. The writer says:—

"The brig B. G. Chaloner, of East Machias, Me., was
chartered in New York to come to Statilla Mills, on the Statilla river, to load lumber. Capt. A. V. Kinney was master,
who had with him his wife, Mr. Patterson the mate, and a
crew of four men.

"Mr. Patterson was well acquainted with the river, having
once been wrecked up White Oak Creek. At that time,
while stripping the vessel, he lived with a wealthy planter,
who became much attached to him. No sooner had his
planter friend—Mr. Morrissey—learned that he was again
on the river, than he sent a negro to conduct him to the
house. Mr. Morrissey, learning that the Captain had his
wife with him, sent a pressing invitation by Mr. Patterson for
the Captain to come, and bring his wife with him, to take a
Christmas dinner with his family.

"On Sunday morning, Dec. 25th, the Captain, with his
wife and mate, took the crew in the boat and started for Mr.
Morrissey's plantation, having to go about fifteen miles by
water to his place of landing, from which, to the plantation,
was five miles. After landing, he sent his men to Mr. Pe-
ters' house, (he being acquainted with Mr. P.,) to tarry until
his return. The crew had been in the house but a short time
when six armed men came there, by the names of David
Brown, and his two sons, Burrill Brown and Nathan Brown,
with their brother-in-law, Thomas Harrison, and two others
whose names I don't recollect, and told them they must go to
jail. The sailors, believing their innocence would appear the
more apparent if they yielded, concluded to obey their orders,
supposing they were authoritative. They were then taken
into the woods, tied to a tree, and a negro made to give three
of them *fifty* lashes apiece. The reserved one was a tall
man, of the height of six feet three inches, whom they called
'the captain of the crowd.' Upon his back, they dealt *one*

hundred lashes. After he was taken down, they asked him if he would run as fast as the others had—they having been compelled to run as fast as released. As he did not at once start, one of the gang raised his gun, saying, '—— you, you won't run, won't you?' and fired, the ball passing near his head, and lodging in a tree. With what strength remained, the suffering man then started, hastened by the profane threats of his menacing tormentors. By the kindness of Burrill Brown's wife, the men were shown the way down, and a boat was provided to take them on board the vessel.

"On Monday morning, as Capt. Kinney, his wife, and Mr. Patterson were coming down toward the landing, they were met by the men who took the sailors aboard, and told what had happened, and advised to go back to Mr. Morrissey's and leave the woman, and then go round the other way and send a sheriff for the boat. This advice was acted upon. They had not gone more than half a mile before they were over-taken by a man on horseback, who pointed a double-barrelled gun at the captain's head, and told him to stop. Presently, old Brown and his gang came along, armed with pistols and guns, and ordered the captain and mate to take off their coats, which they refused to do. Guns were at once cocked and levelled at their heads, and compliance demanded by threat-ening to blow out their brains.

"After they had divested themselves of their outer gar-ments, a negro was ordered to give them *fifty* lashes apiece. The captain's wife piteously interceded in behalf of her hus-band and companion, but they coarsely told her to stop her d—d crying, or they would give her the same number of lashes they were now giving her husband. After the negro had completed his task, old Brown, who was unable to walk without a cane, came hobbling along, and commanded the slave to give them four more for tally.

"The six inquisitors then marched the sufferers before their guns to the boat, and shoved it off, leaving them to row fif-teen miles, against the tide, to their vessel.

"A few days after the transaction, the mate showed me his back, which was bruised and cut from his neck to his knees, as was also the case with the others who were flogged.

"The only reason given for committing this outrage was, that the captain and his men were 'damned Northerners.'"

A METHODIST CLERGYMAN IMPRISONED.

We have to-day to add another to the already long catalogue of outrages on the liberty of speech committed in behalf of slavery.

Rev. Mr. Howe, a Methodist clergyman in Harrison Co., Missouri, was challenged by a Kentuckian neighbor to debate the slavery question. He accepted the challenge in good faith, and the debate took place, with no unusual circumstances, about six miles from Bethany, the county seat. Immediately afterwards, Mr. Howe was arrested. A man owning $3,000 worth of slaves had made affidavit that he was "an Abolitionist," and demanded his incarceration in the penitentiary. A prosecution so evidently malicious and absurd did not alarm Mr. Howe until his return to town, when he found that all the lawyers, with one exception, had *combined* to refuse to defend him. Out of this combination were selected W. G. Lewis, Circuit Attorney, and J. W. Wyatt, to conduct the prosecution. The one exception was O. L. Abbott, Esq., a native of this State, and a graduate of the Albany Law School. He undertook Mr. Howe's defence, but was allowed no time for preparation. Notwithstanding he offered, in behalf of the prisoner, any amount of bail, and asked that the examination might be postponed, he was compelled to go on immediately, without having had an hour's time to ascertain the nature of the case or obtain evidence, and that, too, in regard to an offence hitherto unknown to the record of crime!

During the examination, the court sustained every objection made by the prosecuting attorneys to questions which were all-important to the interests of the defence. The defendant was required to produce all the testimony in his behalf in court at midnight! At one o'clock, however, the judge, for his own convenience, having other business coming on in the morning, consented to a postponement for two days. In the mean time, all the influences that could be exerted to embarrass the defence were resorted to.

When the trial was resumed, the town was filled with people from all parts of the county. The large court room was densely crowded. The evidence closed late in the afternoon.

Mr. Abbott summed up his case, assisted, since no lawyer would assist him, by Rev. John S. Allen, who, though a slaveholder himself, was not willing to see his town disgraced by such tyranny against free speech. Judge Lewis followed in a fanatical pro-slavery tirade against the prisoner, his counsel, "incendiaries" and "Abolitionists" in general, and the case was submitted for decision.

That decision will be looked for with interest, even at this distance from the scene. The crime with which Mr. Howe is charged is defined as "uttering words, the tendency of which is to excite any slave to insolence and insubordination," [Missouri R. S., vol. 1, p. 536,] although it was shown in evidence that there was not a negro, bond or free, within two miles of the place of debate! The penalty for this offence is five years' imprisonment at hard labor in the penitentiary.

During and since the trial, threats have been freely made of "tar and feathers" against the prisoner's counsel, and various attempts made to intimidate and drive him from the place.—*Albany Evening Journal, March* 7.

THE REIGN OF TERROR IN MISSOURI.

To the Editor of the New York Tribune:

Sir,—In the *Tribune* of Jan. 6, you publish a letter of mine to Mr. Anthon, of New York, which has caused great excitement here, and subjected me and others to much abuse.

My son, Robert Milliken, graduated last June at Antioch College, in Ohio, and established a school here the 6th day of last month, and was doing well. He gave general satisfaction until my letter to Mr. Anthon was published in the paper here. Suspicion was fastened on him as the author of the letter, and the pro-slavery men, alias the Democrats, commenced threatening to break up his school. His assistant, a young man by the name of Ira Chamberlain, was violently assaulted at a public meeting, and struck a blow on the head. Notwithstanding I came out and avowed myself the author of the letter, and they poured out a flood of abuse on me, they do not abate their persecution of my son.

Yesterday, a Methodist clergyman called upon him, and told him that money would not hire him (the clergyman) to stand in my son's place; for, said the clergyman, your life is in danger. I hope and trust that he was mistaken. I am sure that if whiskey were let alone, there would be no danger. I have been informed by some Free-State men, who have not openly avowed their Free-State sentiments, and consequently mingle with the pro-slavery squads who are engaged in discussing this matter, that the pro-slavery men threaten to make me leave the State. What the result will be is difficult to conjecture, but I think they will hardly carry matters thus far. Still, it is hard to say what men will not do when intoxicated with modern Democracy and pro-slaveryism.

I live out of town, and have had nothing to say on political matters since I came here, for the reason that all my time has been employed in improving my farm, having made improvements costing over $2,000. It is true, when asked what party I acted with, I have answered, with the Republican, which is nearly enough to forfeit all rights as a citizen. So, there is no feeling against me except for my politics, and this letter to Mr. Anthon.

At a public meeting held at the court-house in Kirksville, the Democrats read extracts from the "Compend," and denounced the book and me in no measured terms. What I regretted the most was, they read extracts that I could not endorse. When I get the book and read it for myself, and not have it dealt out to me in garbled extracts, it may put a different face on these passages. They could hardly find words strong enough to show their hatred to that part of the book that advises non-slaveholders not to patronize slaveholders, and all who endorsed such procedure by circulating the book. Now, the very next morning, these same men went to work in good earnest to break up my son's school, who had circulated no Compends, but simply because I had written that letter, and that he was an anti-slavery man. They have succeeded in driving half of his scholars from his school.

To show the strong efforts they made to break up his school, I will here copy a letter that he received from one of his patrons:—

"Mr. Robert Milliken:

Dear Sir,—It is with regret that I take my son from your school. It is not because of your political views, or any disrespect I have for you or any of the family, but I want to live in friendship with all men, and my friends are falling out with me. I could not send him much longer any how. To save difficulty with other men, I will take him away. Don't think hard of me.

"Yours, with respect,   ————."

The author of the letter told a neighbor that he was in danger of being mobbed if he did not take his son out of school. Look into these statements, and you can see the men who are so shocked and outraged at Helper's advice to non-slaveholders not to patronize slaveholders.

Slavery has crushed the spirit of '76 in all the slave States. Since I came to Missouri, I have been astonished to see the restraint it exercised over free-labor men from the free States. To hear them say, "I know that slavery is a curse, but it will not do to say so publicly," makes one feel that the patriots of the Revolution bled in vain for the rights secured to us in the Constitution of the United States, for their unworthy posterity are about to yield them up to satisfy the demands of slavery.

Yours, truly,

JAS. P. MILLIKEN.

Kirksville, Jan. 28, 1860.

————

Exclusion of Free Negroes from Mississippi. The bill for excluding free negroes from the State of Mississippi passed the House on the 7th December, by a vote of 75 to 5. It provides that they shall leave the State on or before the 1st of July, 1860; or, if they prefer to remain, that they shall be sold into slavery, with a right of choice of masters at a price assessed by three disinterested slaveholders, the proceeds to go into the treasury of the county in which the provisions of the bill may require to be executed.

ASSAULT ON HON. MR. HICKMAN.

The Hon. Mr. Edmundson, of Virginia, is well known as a most courteous and unexceptionable gentleman. But under a very quiet demeanor, he carries a chivalrous estimate of the respect due to his own personal honor and the good name of the State to which he belongs.

So it chanced a few days since, as the Hon. Mr. Hickman was leaving the House of Representatives, he was followed and accosted by Mr. Edmundson, who held him to account for the slanders uttered by him against the State and people of Virginia.

Just as Mr. Hickman said, " I did not mean to " ———— his disclaimer was cut short by a slap in the face from Mr. Edmundson, accompanied with the emphatic assertion that Mr. Hickman was a " d——d scoundrel." At this moment, Messrs. Keitt and Clingman, who were leaving the Capitol at the same time, seeing from Edmundson's manner that he intended to chastise Hickman, and knowing that they would be placarded in the *Tribune* next day for a conspiracy to beat an unprotected free-soiler, ran up and seized Mr. Edmundson, who struggled very violently to inflict further indignities upon the affrighted Timour.

According to our information, Hickman's hat had been knocked off, and he had staggered back with an aspect and attitude of the most abject alarm. Mr. Keitt cried out in a loud voice to Mr. Hickman, " Pick up your hat and go away ; *we can't hold this man all day !* " and added to Mr. Breckenridge, who was passing at the moment, " Take him along." The bewildered Hickman collected his hat and mechanically obeyed the conservative counsel, and soon, like one of the discomfitted heroes in Homer, " ascended the Black ships," or took refuge in some Republican stronghold. Nor has he been since heard from, so far as we are advised, by cartel, military proclamation, or otherwise. — *Washington States.*

The Washington correspondent of the New York *Evening Post* gives the following account of this disgraceful affair : —

" The attack upon Mr. Hickman on Friday evening by Edmundson, of Virginia, creates a good deal of excitement

among the opposition members. The attack was entirely unprovoked, and was made by a large, stout man, accompanied
by two of his friends, upon a weak, slight, sick man, who was
alone. Mr. Hickman was walking down the Capitol steps,
when Edmundson approached him, saying: 'You made a
speech the other night at Willard's Hotel.' 'I did,' replied
Mr. Hickman. 'And d——n you, you slandered my State,
you liar and coward,' continued Edmundson,   the same
moment striking him with his cane across the head. Mr.
Hickman was about to repel the assault, when he was caught
by Vice President Breckenridge, who led him away; Keitt,
and Bouligny, of New Orleans, taking care of Edmundson.
It is reported that Keitt called out to Breckenridge, alluding
to Hickman, 'Take *the hound* away!'

  "It will be remembered that both Keitt and Edmundson
were the instigators of the attack upon Sumner, and stood
sentinel while Brooks did his bloody work. No one thinks
Mr. Keitt had any thing to do with the recent outrage except
to separate the parties. I understand that Mr. Hickman bled
at the lungs freely the night and morning after the brutal attack upon him. It was remarked yesterday that Mr. Breckenridge was in the House for half an hour, and all the time
he sat laughing with Edmundson, who, overcoat on and cigar
in his mouth, sat upon one of the sofas in the extremity of
the hall, and finally the Vice President went out with his
Virginia friend, as if he meant to testify to the House his ap-
probation of the attack on Mr. Hickman. It must be remembered that the brutal attack was unprovoked, and if the
excuse be offered for Edmundson that he was tipsy, it will be
replied that when sober he offered no apology. I think it is
safe to say that the offence will not again be repeated this
winter, for every Republican member will henceforth be prepared for any assault, at any time, even at the breakfast and
dinner table; for Southern gentlemen choose most singular
places and occasions to attack Northern representatives."

———

  A BLACKSMITH DRIVEN AWAY. Benjamin F. Winter, a
blacksmith by trade, has been ordered to leave the town of
Hamilton, Harris County, Ga., by a meeting of citizens, for
avowing Abolition and incendiary sentiments.

MORE SOUTHERN FANATICISM.

On Monday last, Marshal McDonald brought before the Vigilance Committee two men, named Manchester and Bishop. About the first of December last, the Vigilance Committee examined two young men who were procuring subscriptions to the American Cyclopædia. It was charged on them that they had been tampering with slaves. The Committee not deeming the evidence against them sufficient to authorize summary punishment, they were discharged, with the injunction to leave the State, and to abandon their agency, and inform the publishers or their agents that the book should not be delivered in this county, the Committee at that time thinking they were agents for Appleton's "New American Cyclopædia," which had been condemned by Mr. Pryor, and which was regarded by the Committee as being incendiary in its tendency.

The two men, Manchester and Bishop, notwithstanding the warning given to Smith and Tilden, undertook to sell them, whereupon they were arrested, and upon examination, a book was found in their possession entitled "Cotton is King," which, after a careful perusal by Dr. W. S. Price, R. S. Wier, and ourself, who were appointed a Committee for that purpose, was reported as being incendiary and of a dangerous character.

It was further shown in evidence against them, that they had sold and circulated said book in this county and Newton. After much discussion as to what action the Committee should take in the premises, the vote was taken, when six present voted to turn them over to the authorities, and five voted to treat them to a coat of tar and feathers. The majority ruling, they were then turned over to R. T. Kennedy, Esq., who committed them to the county jail, to answer at the spring term of our Circuit Court.

A strong feeling on the part of the citizens to tar and feather them was manifested, and, as for our part, we think that the proper way to deal with such men. The books were burned in the street.—*Enterprise (Miss.) News.*

A CHIVALROUS DEMONSTRATION.

Albertis Patterson, a citizen of West Finley township, in this county, happened to be at Haineytown, a small village in Virginia, situated near the line that divides that State from this county, on or about the 25th ult., and was accosted by three of the chivalrous citizens of that region, named Seaton, Caldwell and Wherry, and interrogated as to his political opinions. He replied that he was a Know-Nothing, when his interrogators charged him with being a "Black Republican or Abolitionist," and asked him if he did not sympathize with John Brown. To this he answered that he *was* a Republican; and as for John Brown, he "believed that Gov. Wise was as big a fool as he was." Upon making this declaration, he was violently seized by Seaton and Caldwell, a rope was procured, looped and thrown around his neck, and the desperadoes immediately proceeded to strangle him, which they most unquestionably would have succeeded in doing had it not been for the interference of two men, named Armstrong and Bemer, who happened to be on the street at the time. When Patterson was rescued from his brutal assailants, his face was black from strangulation, and his neck bruised and discolored by the abrasion of the rope.

The scoundrels, we are sorry to say, escaped unpunished; but should any such demonstrations be made in future by the chivalry of that region, we are assured the ruffians will be hanged to the nearest limb. They will find that Haineytown is not Charlestown, although both villages are within the jurisdiction of the Old Dominion, where every petty postmaster and country squire is, *ex officio*, inquisitor of the opinions of his neighbor. But Haineytown catches some of the healthy breezes of independence from our western boundary, and it is not quite a safe experiment there to choke people to death, even for believing that his late Excellency, Gov. Wise, is a little weak in the upper story.— *Washington* (*Pa.*) *Tribune.*

In Charlottesville, Va., a man from the North, named Rood, has been arrested on suspicion, and papers found on him sufficiently important to warrant his imprisonment.

Two Young Ladies Driven Out of Richmond. Two intelligent young ladies, formerly well known in the choirs of churches in Boston and Hartford, went to Richmond in September last with a view of establishing a private school. They soon gained the confidence of many friends, and succeeded in starting an enterprise which gave fair prospect of speedily prospering. As soon as the recent excitement began, they were waited upon by some very respectable gentlemen, who informed them that Northern school-mistresses, however amiable and competent, were not the proper persons to teach the children of Southern parents and guardians! The ladies were forced immediately to break up their school. Wishing, on account of their health, to remain in a Southern climate, and hearing of a vacancy in a school in another city in Virginia, they made application and presented their letters. They received a reply from a clergyman, who wrote to them as follows: —

"The Board of Trustees met yesterday, and passed upon the various applications, yours among the rest. I deeply regret to say, that although your recommendations were altogether the most favorable, your proposal was immediately rejected, as soon as the fact became known that you were both from the North. The feeling is so strong, and the foolish excitement has run so high, on the subject of Northern people, that the community here seem almost blind; and if they continue in their present policy, they will lay themselves open to severe criticism, if not to censure."

Accordingly, the ladies, being compelled to leave Richmond, and unable to find a place for the soles of their feet any where else in Virginia, and knowing the uselessness of going further south, took an early train to New York. One of them still remains in this city, where she is anxious to procure a situation as soprano singer in a choir, or as a teacher of music to private pupils. Any application sent to her through the office of the *Independent*, addressed "Richmond," will be immediately forwarded to her. The name of Mr. Horace Waters, music publisher, is among her references. — *New York Independent*.

———

Pushed Off a Railroad Car. A passenger on the Mississippi Central Railroad was pushed off the train while it was in full motion, for denouncing Gov. Wise and lauding John Brown.

EXPULSION OF FREE NEGROES FROM ARKANSAS. At the late session of the Arkansas Legislature, an act was passed giving the free negroes of that State the alternative of migrating before January 1st, 1860, or of becoming slaves. As the time of probation has now expired, while some few individuals have preferred servitude, the great body of the free colored people of Arkansas are on their way northward. We learn that the upward bound boats are crowded with them, and that Seymour, Ind., on the line of the Ohio and Mississippi Railroad, affords a temporary home for others.

A party of forty, mostly women and children, arrived in this city last evening by the Ohio and Mississippi Railroad. They were welcomed by a committee of ten, appointed from the colored people of the city, by whom the refugees were escorted to the Dumas House, on McAllister street, at which place a formal reception was held. They were assured by the Chairman of the Reception Committee, Peter H. Clark, that if they were industrious and exemplary in their conduct, they would be sure to gain a good livelihood and many friends. The exiles, as before stated, are mostly women and children, the husbands and fathers being held in servitude. They report concerning the emigration, that hundreds of the free colored men of Arkansas have left for Kansas, and hundreds more are about to follow. — *Cincinnati Gazette, Jan. 4th.*

TWO HEADS HALF-SHAVEN. The steamer Huntsville, which arrived in New York from Savannah, on Monday, Dec. 19th, brought several passengers who had been driven away from different parts of the South. Among them were *two gentlemen whose heads were shaved on one side !* They had been exiled from the chivalrous State of South Carolina ! One of the victims avowed his determination speedily to return to execute vengeance on his maltreaters.

At Danville, Va., a clerk in the Post Office saw a man throw a letter, which he had just gotten, into the stove, and, on taking it out, found it to be a proposition for running off slaves. The man was arrested.

How Two Organ-Grinders were Tarred and Feathered.
— We have private intelligence from a friend in Alabama of
a case of tar and feathering which is both serious and comical.
Two Italian organ-grinders, who could scarcely speak a word
of English, made their way from Mobile into the interior of
the State, to earn a livelihood by itinerating with their poor
tunes. After playing in a bar-room in a small town, and
gathering all the pennies which Southern generosity was likely
to bestow upon such entertainment, they asked to be directed
to the next town. Whereupon, a wag took a piece of paper,
and, under pretence of writing down the necessary direction,
gave the poor men a fatal letter, somewhat as follows : —

"To the Knowing Ones:
"Pass my Italian friends. All right. Mum's the word.
(Signed)   "JOHN BROWN, of Osawatomie."

The music peddlers, on reaching the next town, faint and
weary with the weight of their organs on their backs, went
immediately to a tavern, and unwittingly presented their letter of recommendation ! They were at once taken by the
whiskey drinkers, stripped, threatened until they were terrified
out of their wits, tarred and feathered, and ridden out of town
on a rail ! Such is Southern chivalry !

The New York Independent Outlawed. A correspond-
ent in Texas, who has for years received the *Independent*, has
written to us to stop it, as the continued sending *might cost
him his business and possibly his neck*. No Northern publica-
tions but the New York *Herald* and the Nassau street Tracts
are now considered safe reading on the other side of the line.
— *New York Independent.*

Narrowly Escaped Lynching. An Italian grocer, named
John Ginochio, narrowly escaped being lynched by the citizens
of Petersburg, Va., last Monday, for saying that John Brown
was a good and very useful man, and, instead of being hung,
he ought to have been made President of the United States.

Mr. J. P. Gillespie, of New Albany, Indiana, publishes a card in the *Ledger*, of that city, in which he explains the circumstances connected with a recent visit which he made to Franklin, La., for the purpose of practising his profession. On his arrival there, it became noised about that he was an Abolitionist. A committee waited on him and advised him to leave the place forthwith if he wished to escape lynching. Mr. G. denied the accusation. A large crowd assembled around the hotel to carry out the threat, and Mr. G. armed himself and walked out into the crowd, demanding to know the person who made the accusation. Capt. Atkinson was given as the author, who had said that he (Gillespie) had gone into Kentucky, with an armed band of men, to rescue a "nigger" thief by the name of Bell, and that they had carried off some slaves at the same time. Mr. Gillespie left on the following day on a steamer for Berwick Bay, and then for New Orleans, accompanied by a number of persons from Franklin, who pointed him out as an Abolitionist. Immediately on his arrival at New Orleans, he took passage on an up-river boat.

We learn that Rev. George Candee, Rev. Wm. Kendrick, and Robert Jones, missionaries of the American Missionary Association, in Jackson County, Ky., (Jones, a colporteur,) were recently, near Laurel, where they were preaching, waited upon by a committee of five, and requested to leave. They were engaged to preach the next morning, but were prevented by a mob, which took them a half mile and interrogated them, then took them five miles further and left them, after shaving their hair and beards, and putting tar on their heads and faces. Mr. Kendrick was in the Union Theological Seminary of this city last year. — *New York Independent*.

The Sylvania (Georgia) *News* reports that two book agents were treated to thirty-nine lashes each, after the style of "Russian executioners," by a planter in that vicinity, recently, because they had visited his plantation and rendered themselves not only disagreeable by their volubility, but suspicious by their conduct.

5

LEGISLATION IN MARYLAND.

They have a most iniquitous way of legislating on some subjects in the State of Maryland. The Commmittee on Corporations of the House of Delegates recently had an investigation into alleged frauds in the passage of the City Passenger Railway Ordinance of the city of Baltimore. Among the witnesses was Mr. Jonathan Brock, and he was questioned after the following manner. We are not able to see exactly what this has to do with railroads, but we suppose the Maryland Legislature could tell : —

Q. — Will you state whether you have any Black Republican proclivities? A. — I have not. I do not belong to that crowd. Q. — Did you ever know Passmore Williamson? A. — I do not. I would not know him, if I saw him. Q. — You never, of course, engaged in any effort to rescue him from the grasp of the law, or from punishment? A. — No, sir. Q. — Do you know whether your associates, or any of them, are Black Republicans? A. — I do not think they are; they are not politicians. Mr. Grove is an American, and sometimes takes part with the opposition. Q. — To what party do you belong? A. — The old line Whig. I have not meddled with politics since 1844; it would not do well. I am engaged in business in Florida. Q. — You mentioned Mr. Miller, of Pennsylvania. What is he; an American, or a Democrat? A. — A Democrat. He was Clerk of the Senate. Q. — No Black Republican? A. — I don't think he is. Q. — And none of your people are tainted with it? A. — They are all Union men. Q. — It has even been charged that your wife is some connection of Lucretia Mott; did you ever see her? A. — I have seen her. Q. — Does she know you? A. — No, sir. Q. — Does your wife know her? A. — She knows her in the street, but she is no connection of hers, and no acquaintance. Q. — Your road is never used to run off negroes from Baltimore? A. — No, sir, and never shall. Q. — Has SIMON CAMERON directly or indirectly any interest in this road? A. — He has not. Q. — Is it understood that he is to have any, or his friends? A. — There is no promise; no understanding. He is with the other side. Q. — He and you are not friendly? A. — No, sir. Q. — You are antagonistic?

A.—He is here, endeavoring to get this grant after the passage of it. Q.—Is the party of which the counsel spoke known as the Black Republican or Republican party? A.—In some States, it is called the Opposition party. Q.—When was the last State election in Pennsylvania? A.—In October. Q.—Where were you at the time? A.—I do not recollect whether I was in Pennsylvania, or not. Q.—Did you vote? A.—I do not recollect that; I am not positive. Q.—Who were the candidates for State officers? A.—I do not know; I took no part in politics. Q.—Did you vote in 1856? A.—I did not vote for President, in 1856. Q.—Have you voted since the party, known as the Republican party, has been in existence? A.—It is not called the Republican party in our State. Q.—The Opposition, then? A.—I have. Q.—How did you vote then? A.—I voted a mixed ticket—for my personal friends—I did not care whether they were Americans or Democrats. Q.—Have you voted for a Congressman since that time? A.—I presume I have, but really, I do not know who the candidates were, I tell you plainly. Q.—If a Democratic Congressman were running, and an Opposition candidate, which one would you vote for? A.—Whichever was my personal friend. Q.—Suppose neither was? A.—I can't tell; I have no decided politics. Q.—Was, or was not one of your associates elected to the City Council in a Black Republican ward? A.—I do not know that one was elected.

———

WHITE FAMILIES LEAVING VIRGINIA. The New York *Times* says that it has reliable information when it states that, in consequence of the Harper's Ferry affair, the heavy property-holders of Virginia begin to see that the subject of slavery is destined to produce interminable strife in that State in the future, and materially decrease the value of property. Families are accordingly preparing to leave the State; panic pervades all classes of citizens; there is no freedom of speech; suspicion and distrust are abroad; the last resort to check the progress of crime, the jury system, has become weak and corrupt; the spirit of religion is dying out, and infidelity taking its place. The country, according to this representation, is in fact but one degree removed from anarchy.

A TEACHER EXPELLED FROM ARKANSAS.

Correspondence of the Chicago Tribune.

AURORA, Illinois, Feb. 15th, 1860.

With your permission, I will occupy a small space in your paper, as a witness against the tyranny and oppression in the South. I have resided in Louisiana and Arkansas over ten years, was engaged in teaching, and am an official member of the Methodist Episcopal Church.

Since the Harper's Ferry affair, the Southern people have a peculiar hatred against Northern and Eastern people, irrespective of party.

In January, a spy was sent to me to ascertain my political views, endeavoring to extort from me a confession that "slavery was a social, moral and political blessing," (or sentiments to that amount,) and also to have me enlist in a military company, to be ready "to fight the North, and particularly the Yankees, in the next expected outbreak"; to "be ready to fight for the dissolution of the Union," &c.

I informed the spy that "I could not, consistently with my convictions of right and wrong," and further, "*I would not!*" that "I was proud of Yankeedom as the land of my nativity, and that I would sooner die than take up arms against my parents, brothers and sisters."

Three days after, I was waited upon by a gentleman slaveholder, showing me resolutions, signed by nearly all the planters in that vicinity, resolving themselves into a "Vigilance Committee, for the security of their slaves, pledging themselves one to another to examine every non-slaveholder, and satisfy themselves beyond a doubt of the soundness of every person; and should they find any one of whom they should have the slightest suspicion, they would communicate at once one with another."

The gentleman then accused me of receiving Abolition literature, saying that a *Congregational Herald* was found at the post-office addressed to me, and that I had correspondence and associations in the North and East. This I admitted; also that "I was anti-slavery from the bottom of my heart." He then notified me "to leave within thirty-six hours; that he would protect me that length of time, but he would not promise me my life to be safe any longer." I consented to leave rather than lose my life. I was obliged to leave all my property, library and all, not being allowed time to collect my claims or pay my debts, or to talk with any *non*-slaveholder — breaking up my school, and throwing me out of employment.

I have reason to praise God that I am once more free, in a land where the truth is not muzzled, where free discussion is tolerated, and that I have emerged from that savage wilderness where reigns the prince of darkness, whose haunts are commanded by slaveholders and dealers in human flesh, where, as long as life shall last, and I have the power of expression, and as long as I can wield a pen, I shall bear testimony against that debasing system which is oppressing so many millions of our human race.

Thanks be to God that there is a party in the North, the great Republican party, that great terror to the South, who are riding forth to conquer, whose great moral influence is being felt in all the remotest parts of slavedom.

Respectfully,

H. T. TEWKSBURY.

———

FRIGHTENED BY A BLIND GIRL. The Wheeling (Va.) *Intelligencer* publishes the statement of a blind girl, who was recently expelled from Martinsburgh, Va., on suspicion of being an Abolitionist. She says: "Some of the people treated me kindly enough, but the lady of the house insisted that I was an Abolitionist; that coming as I did from Indiana, I was not entitled to belief. A gentleman came into my room uninvited and questioned me in an impudent manner. I applied to a minister, who said he would be glad to assist me, but would advise me *not* to stay during the excitement. It was in consequence of this that I was compelled to leave." In addition to this, the conductor of the train upon which the blind lady and her sister arrived, told us, in the presence of a number of gentlemen, that the ladies were not permitted to remain. He was asked if he knew them, and upon replying that he did not, was told that "they could not stay there."

A correspondent of a Richmond paper makes the following offer : —

"$100,000 REWARD. — MESSRS. EDITORS, — I will be one of one hundred gentlemen, who will give twenty-five dollars each *for the heads of the following traitors:*

"Henry Wilson, Massachusetts; Charles Sumner, Massachusetts; Horace Greeley, New York; John P. Hale, New Hampshire; Wendell Phillips, Henry Ward Beecher, Brooklyn; Rev. Dr. Cheever, New York; Rev. Mr. Wheelock, New Hampshire; Schuyler Colfax, Anson Burlingame, Owen Lovejoy, Amos P. Granger, Edwin B. Morgan, Galusha A. Grow, Joshua R. Giddings, Edward Wade, Calvin C. Chaffee, William H. Kelsey, William A. Howard, Henry Waldron, John Sherman, George W. Palmer, Daniel W. Gooch, Henry L. Dawes, Justin S. Morrill, I. Washburn, Jr., J. A. Bingham, William Kellogg, E. B. Washburn, Benjamin Stanton, Edward Dodd, C. B. Tompkins, John Covode, Cad. C. Washburn, Samuel G. Andrews, A. B. Olin, Sidney Dean, N. B. Durfee, Emory B. Pottle, DeWitt C. Leach, J. F. Potter, T. Davis, Massachusetts; T. Davis, Iowa; J. F. Farnsworth, C. L. Knapp, R. E. Fenton, Philemon Bliss, Mason W. Tappan, Charles Case, James Pike, Homer E. Boyce, Isaac D. Clawson, A. S. Murray, Robert B. Hall, Valentine B. Horton, Freeman H. Morse, David Kilgore, William Stewart, Samuel B. Curtis, John M. Wood, John M. Parker, Stephen C. Foster, Charles J. Gilman, C. B. Hoard, John Thompson, J. W. Sherman, William D. Braxton, James Buffington, O. B. Matteson, Richard Mott, George K. Robbins, Ezekiel P. Walton, James Wilson, S. A. Purviance, Francis E. Spinner, Silas M. Burroughs. And I will also be one of one hundred to pay five hundred dollars each ($50,000) *for the head of William H. Seward,* and would add a similar reward for Fred. Douglass, but regarding him head and shoulders above these traitors, will permit him to remain where he now is.

"RICHMOND."

An exhibition of wax figures, including the Savior and the Apostles, and John Brown, was burned by a mob at Milton, Florida, recently.

EXPULSION OF TWO MECHANICS. The Lafayette (In.) *Journal* has the following incident: "Two well known citizens of Lafayette, Freeman Patt and Henry Frounfelter, were driven out of Louisiana, a few days ago, on suspicion of entertaining Abolition sentiments. The two were brickmasons, and had gone there to build a sugar-house for a planter living sixty miles from New Orleans. After having worked about two weeks, they were waited upon by the planter and informed that their services were no longer required. They inquired the cause of dismissal, but received no satisfaction, further than a request to leave as soon as possible. It being near evening, and the steamboat landing about five miles from the plantation, they requested the privilege of remaining until morning, which was refused. They then proceeded to the landing, escorted by a number of persons armed to the teeth, who waited until a boat came along, when they were hurried on board, and admonished to leave the State, and not return. The hint was taken, and the two gentlemen arrived here on Wednesday night, thoroughly disgusted with life at the South.

A PHILADELPHIA DRUMMER MENACED. The Griffin (Ga.) *Democrat* says: "A drummer from the house of H. Bancroft & Co., Philadelphia, by the name of Gonnally, insulted a gentleman connected with one of our business houses, a few days since, by the use of language not altogether understood, but, interpreted, meant opposition to slavery. The drummer, finding he had picked up the wrong customer, made an apology satisfactory to the injured party, and thereby escaped a severe flagellation, which he, no doubt, deserved. Some of these drummers have the impudence of Old Nick. It will do no harm to watch them all. Our motto, when one of them insults a Southern man, upon Southern soil, is to show him no mercy, under any circumstances, until he learns to treat with respect the rights and property of those he seeks to make money out of by a regular system of espionage in divers ways. For ourselves, we are sick and tired of submission in such cases. One or two examples of the right kind would produce a radical change in a short time. The 'Q. V. X. Q.'s' should be on the look out. They may have some fun."

TREASONABLE LINEN.   We have seen a private correspondence from a Northern gentleman now travelling in the Southern States, which states that a very worthy and quiet mechanic from New England was driven away from a village in Georgia, because his valise contained a clean shirt, wrapped up in a copy of the New York *Sun*, containing Henry Ward Beecher's sermon on the Harper's Ferry affair.   Whether the Georgians objected to the clean shirt or the paper is not stated; but as the *Sun* is in the interest of the pro-slavery Democracy, we presume the shirt was the occasion of their anger.   The test of party affiliation appears to be the same at the South as at the North — clean linen being *prima facie* evidence of Republicanism, and the contrary of Democracy. — *Grand Rapids (Mich.) Eagle.*

A TRAP TO CATCH HON. JOSHUA R. GIDDINGS.   A correspondent of the Cincinnati *Commercial*, who has lately visited Richmond, writes from Mayfield, Ky., that while in Kentucky, he learned of a deep-laid scheme to capture J. R. Giddings, for the purpose of trying him for treason, etc., in view of his connection with the Harper's Ferry insurgents.   This scheme is founded upon the reward offered recently, anonymously, for the bringing of his person to Virginia.   This amount has been raised for this purpose, and the object will be to seize him and cross the line into Kentucky and Virginia immediately.   The correspondent, who writes anonymously, says further :   " I would have addressed Mr. Giddings directly, but do not know his post-office.   I would advise him to be ever on his guard, and keep as far from the Ohio river as possible.   I offer no apology for not giving my name, living as I do in the South."

A young man named Baker, formerly an organist and daguerreotypist at Rome, New York, and son of Rev. Mr. Baker, of Utica, was lately driven from Augusta, Georgia. Mr. Baker went to Augusta to take the position of organist in an Episcopal Church, and had played but one Sabbath, when he was warned to leave, or submit to a coat of tar and feathers.

SUMMARY LYNCHING AT CHAPPELL'S DEPOT, SOUTH CARO-
LINA. A fearful tragedy was enacted at Chappell's Depot,
South Carolina, on the morning of February 6th. It seems
that a man calling himself James C. Bungings was observed
prowling about the vicinity for several days, having apparent-
ly no recognized business to detain him in the place. The
Vigilance Committee watched his movements closely.

He was finally tracked, on Sunday night (the 5th), and the
Committee, being satisfied of his evil intentions, arrested him
and upon examination, found any quantity of papers, showing
that he was one of Brown's associates, with a commission to
go into all the South, with a view of corrupting the minds of
the negroes, to make as many converts as possible to the Abolition faith, and to induce as many negroes as possible to de-
camp for the North.

The evidence was deemed sufficient, and he was taken into
custody and detained for the night. In the morning, he was
led forth in front of Chappell's Railroad Depot, and told to
prepare for immediate execution. There were about fifty
persons present, but not one voice was raised to save him
from his terrible doom.

After offering up a long prayer, the wretched man asked
to see a clergyman, but there being none present, he called on
God to forgive the Vigilance Committee, if they were in error ; or if he was the one who erred, to have mercy on his
soul.

He was then mounted on a ladder, a rope with a slip-knot
put round his neck, the other end of which was drawn over
the limb of a tree. At nine o'clock, A. M., the ladder was
knocked from under him, his neck was broken, and in a few
minutes he was dead ! The body was left hanging to the tree
until twelve o'clock, the time at which the passenger train is
due from Columbia. It was then cut down, and the mortal
remains of James C. Bungings were given to the medical
students for dissection.

The Rockville (Md.) *Journal* says that a man was arrested
near the Great Falls, in that county, on Wednesday last, for
the expression of a feeling of sympathy with the late rebellion at Harper's Ferry. He is now in the county jail.

5 *

A SOUTHERN OUTRAGE. A German peddler, named Moses Schlosstein, well known in this place, and who has pursued his business in this region, was the victim recently of a gross outrage in Georgia. He was selling his wares in Merriweather, one of the western counties of the State, about sixteen miles from Greenville, the county seat. He was passing a blacksmith shop, where there was a crowd gathered, and saluted them politely, as traders generally do. But the "non-intercourse" fever forbade them to reciprocate the civility. They seized him, and proceeded to beat him unmercifully. This assault was an outburst of chivalrous feeling, and then, feigning a suspicion of his having "incendiary documents" in his possession, they followed and caught him again. With their knives, they ripped open his pack, cutting his goods to pieces; they then stripped him, beat him outrageously, and left him insensible. When he returned to consciousness, he found that he was cut about the face and body, and that the thumb of the right hand was broken. He gathered together his ruined goods, and fortunately found a fearless and hospitable man, who kept him ten days, when he was able to travel. He is now staying with Mr. Myerson, his relative, in this place. Mr. Schlosstein has been in the habit of voting the Democratic ticket, but he thinks the treatment he has received from his brother Democrats has about induced him to change his mind in that regard.— *Norristown Herald.*

It will be remembered that we published, some weeks since, an account of the sacking of the house of John C. Underwood, of Clarke County, Va., and the assault and wounding with a bayonet of one of the women of that neighborhood, who resisted the entrance of the brutal soldiery into her house, and was thus disabled, in defence of herself and daughters from the licentious and drunken forces of Gov. Wise, in the absence of her husband. We now learn that this woman was the wife of Martin Feltner, a tenant of Mr. Underwood, a most worthy member of the Methodist Church, and the mother of fourteen living children — ten sons and four daughters. We are glad to learn that a contribution is to be made by our citizens as a testimonial to. her courage and virtue. — *New York Tribune.*

ANOTHER OUTRAGE. Mr. David Fuld, clothing dealer, of West Chester, having a claim to collect in Warwick, Cecil county, Md., went down, taking a free colored man, David, along as a carriage driver, when an excited crowd gathered about the house, exclaiming, " Hang the d——d northern nigger," " shoot him," " fine him $150," " fine him $500," and other expressions peculiar to that latitude. A " squire " was in the crowd, and informed Mr. Fuld that the legal fine was $20, and the costs 25 cents. (As no warrant was issued, we suppose this was for the use of the mob.) Mr. Fuld paid the fine, and took a receipt, which the constable endorsed good for five days for the "negro." But his prompt payment seemed to annoy them. They used abusive and insulting language, and swore he should not take the " nigger " back to Pennsylvania. One man offered him $800 for the negro, and he was told that he had better take that than nothing, for he would have to go home without him. Some one suggested that it would be safest to leave, when Mr. F. and his man left, without finishing his business, and returned to Pennsylvania with exalted notions of our " ga-lo-rious " Union!—*Norristown (Pa.) Republican.*

———

METHODISM DANGEROUS IN KENTUCKY. It appears by the Cynthiana *News*, that the members of the Methodist Church, North, in Kentucky, are considered dangerous members of society. The *News* calls the Conference which is to meet at Germantown, Ky., on the 8th of March, Bishop Simpson to preside, an " Abolition Conference," and quotes a denunciation of the Fugitive Slave Law from the *Western Christian Advocate*, when Bishop Simpson was the editor, as evidence that he is a dangerous man, at the head of a dangerous abolition association!

The Methodist Episcopal Church, North, has an Annual Conference in Kentucky, with 24 travelling preachers from Ohio, according to the *News*, and 31 local preachers, and 2,496 laymen, scattered along the Ohio river, from one end of the State to the other. The *News* insists that slaveholders should desist from driving out such small fry as Fee & Co., 'until they can manage " one of the most powerful abolition associations in the world, in our midst!" What next?

A few days ago, two or three gentlemen from Philadelphia took a jaunt to the home and grave of the father of his country, and were studiously watched, as if they had come armed with fire and sword, or as if they were resolved to poison the entire State. On their return, having purchased three canes cut from the homestead of Washington, which they had wrapped in a blanket shawl, they soon discovered that they had become objects of suspicion, and it became necessary for them to explain that they carried no deadly weapons. Bear in mind that the large Mount Vernon fund has been begged principally out of the North.

GEORGIA. The Legislature of Georgia has passed a law, making it unlawful hereafter for any itinerant person or persons to vend or sell in that State any article of value, not manufactured in Georgia, by sample or otherwise, without a license. The license is " one hundred dollars, or other sum, at the discretion of the Inferior Court of the county" in which the peddling or sales are made. An additional tax of one per cent. on one hundred dollars sold is imposed. The penalty is fine and imprisonment.

A law has also been passed providing that free negroes, wandering or strolling about, or leading an idle, immoral, or profligate course of life, shall be sold into slavery for a period not exceeding two years for the first offence; but upon conviction of a second offence, they must be sold into perpetual slavery.

The Montgomery (Ala.) *Mail*, of Tuesday last, says : — " Last Saturday, we devoted to the flames a large number of copies of Spurgeon's Sermons, and the pile was graced at the top with a copy of ' Graves's Great Iron Wheel,' which a Baptist friend presented for the purpose. We trust that the works of the greasy cockney vociferator may receive the same treatment throughout the South. And if the Pharisaical author should ever show himself in these parts, we trust that a stout cord may speedily find its way around his *eloquent* throat. He has proved himself a dirty, low-bred slanderer, and ought to be treated accordingly."

A METHODIST PREACHER DRIVEN FROM HIS WORK. Benjamin Brown, a colored Methodist preacher, sent by the Conference to labor among the colored people of Milford and Slaughter Neck, was arrested, on Friday last, at the instigation of some of the citizens of Slaughter Neck, for being a non-resident. He was taken before Esq. Revill, who was compelled by the law to due him fifty dollars. He was also ordered to leave the State in five days, or again be subject to fine and imprisonment. It seems, that besides preaching on the Sabbath, he had opened a school, in which free colored children, in great numbers, were learning to read and write; and this excited the opposition that was manifested in enforcing an inhuman law. The preacher is said to be a quiet, peaceable man. His work among the free negroes of this vicinity was elevating and improving them; but to this many white men are opposed, never seeming, while they abuse the negroes for their immoral and vicious practices, to consider that it is their ignorance and degradation that make them so, and to remove which, intelligence and moral elevation is absolutely necessary. Ignorance is the mother of vice, and knowledge is the father of virtue, among all classes of men.

Many of our citizens have since signed a petition to the Judge for this county, for a permit to allow Brown to remain and attend to the duties to which he has been assigned by Bishop Scott; but the Judge has not yet granted it. Brown was ordained a deacon in the church by Bishop Waugh, late of Baltimore, and to Elder's orders by Bishop Baker.

A son of Brown was also engaged in teaching in Milford, but on receiving notification, he left the town, and probably the State.

" Verily I say unto you, inasmuch as ye have done it unto *one of the least of these my brethren, ye have done it unto me.*" — *News and Advertiser, Delaware.*

A correspondent of the Missouri *Republican* says that F. P. Blair was near being arrested by the gensdarmes of Virginia, while eating his dinner at Martinsburg. He was let off, he adds, on giving assurances that he was going to Washington as fast as the locomotive would carry him.

A NEW TEST. The Galena (Ill.) *Advertiser* states that a former resident of that city, a bricklayer, had just returned from Mississippi, where he had found employment at his trade, under the following circumstances. He determined, when settled at the South, to keep his own council with regard to his views upon slavery. Acting upon this course, he managed to glide along smoothly for some time, without molestation. At last, a *new test* was applied to his " sympathies : "

" One rainy day, when the hands were detained in the house, a slave having failed to build as good a fire from green wood as the overseer wanted, the slave was ordered to be thrown down by the latter, and to receive one hundred and fifty lashes, as a punishment. As there was but one room for shelter, our friend was compelled to stand by and see the inhuman cruelty inflicted, or go out and stand in the rain. He promptly chose the latter, and at the end of half or three-quarters of an hour, came in, drenching wet. He was met by a laugh, and a remark by the overseer, that perhaps he did ' not like to see such fun.' His only reply was, that he did not, and nothing more was said on the subject. The next day, a saddled horse was brought up to the door, and he was informed that he could leave that part of the country. He was informed that he could ride into Natchez, and leave the horse and saddle at a particular livery stable. With true British pluck, he refused the service of the animal, and walked to Natchez on foot, and soon made his way back to Galena."

———

A young lady from one of the hill towns of Massachusetts is now teaching in Virginia. After the John Brown affair, notice was given out that she could not have any of her letters from the post-office, until they had been opened and read, in the presence of witnesses, to see if they contained any " incendiary matter." She immediately went to the office, and demanded that her letters should be delivered to her unopened. The Postmaster looked at her a moment, saw that she meant what she said, and delivered her letters to her. She still remains there teaching, unmolested, but says that all that saves her from a coat of tar and feathers is the fact that she is a woman.

WEST CHESTER, Feb. 18, 1860.

MR. WALTER,— As it is two days' journey (sometimes) from this to old Chester, and as long back again, how does it happen that you have beaten all of the four newspapers here, and furnished the Athenians with an account of some of their own doings, before they could tell it themselves? not to speak of giving such fresh news to the benighted "aborigines" just outside, where your paper circulates pretty extensively. I leave this for you to answer at leisure.

A gentleman who left New Orleans in December, told me, a few days ago, that in coming up the great river on a steamboat, they picked up a man who has been a school-teacher, at a certain place in Kansas, for six years past. He had been kindly placed on a log, (to save his life, of course,) and was comfortably furnished with clothing suited to the times, namely, a close-fitting jacket and pants of a dark material you rarely hear of in that direction, and a well-wadded overcoat of that article sometimes treated of in works on ornithology — I like to be brief. His friends had been thus thoughtful to reward him for his sincere endeavors to teach the dark skins how to read and write, as well as in consideration of his six years' faithful services. This gentleman also stated that in passing the mayor's office in Macon, Georgia, he saw about a dozen rails, cushioned at the ends and sharpened in the middle, ready for use at the shortest notice, one with the mayor's mark upon it — doubtless a two-edged one. But enough — as I want to go South some day, I had better close here.

M.

WHOLESALE PROSCRIPTION. In the Oxford (Miss.) *Mercury*, of last week, we find the following:—

"We believe that if the excitement gets much higher, all Northern-born people, of whatever grade, standing, or time they have been living here, will be forced to leave. They never can hope to be considered or treated in the social circle here with the respect once shown to all people of respectability. An Englishman, or any foreign gentleman, is now more highly respected by the people of the South than a Yankee."

ANOTHER EXPULSION FROM KENTUCKY.   Mr. D. B. Hamilton, of Trumbull county, removed from Ohio to Kentucky,
last October, for the purpose of keeping school.   He received
the Western Reserve *Chronicle* regularly, and the New York
Tribune occasionally.   Mr. H. was in Medina on Thursday,
having been driven out of Kentucky by the pro-slavery mob-
ites, for a high misdemeanor, thus related by the *Gazette:* —

"He, on one occasion, took the New York *Tribune* in his
pocket into the school room, and laid it on his desk, and
some of the larger scholars seeing the paper in the school
room, informed the citizens of the fact.   The result was, that
Mr. H. was arrested and tried, for introducing incendiary
reading matter into the public schools, fined one hundred and
fifty dollars and costs of prosecution, and warned to leave the
State immediately.   They kept his wages back to pay his fine,
and drove him off with one dollar in his pocket, leaving his
wife and children behind, not having the means to take them
with him.   Mr. H. is now on his way to Trumbull county, to
raise the means to send for his family.   He has walked all
the way from Kentucky, near five hundred miles, and came
into our town pretty badly used up.   It is not necessary to
make many comments of any kind on such proceedings, but
they will show the freemen of the North what their rights
are, and how much they are respected by the men-drivers of
the southern part of this great republic."

TWO DAYS TO LEAVE THE STATE.   An Abolitionist in Clay-
ton, Alabama, was brought before a meeting of the citizens,
whose sentence was to array him in tar and feathers, and then
ride him on a rail around the town.   The resolution was carried into effect, and the Abolitionist was ordered to leave the
State within two days.

A correspondent of a Charleston (S. C.) paper is highly indignant at what he calls "a clear case of impertinence," viz.:
A Yankee peddler canvassing that city "with the Constitution of the United States in bronze, with gilt frame!"   It is
not the market for any such document as that.

ARREST OF A SUSPICIOUS CHARACTER IN CHARLESTOWN, VIRGINIA. A man, who gives the name of Otis, and claims to hail from the town of Yonkers, New York, was arrested on Saturday, under suspicious circumstances. He made his appearance in the town at a late hour on Friday evening, and put up at the Carter House, and on Saturday he called on Rev. Mr. Waugh with a letter of introduction, which not being satisfactory to the reverend gentleman, he handed him over to the Mayor of the town, who had him placed under guard in one of the rooms of the hotel, where he still remains, but will probably be "shipped" to-day. He has made a variety of statements, one of which is that he had been in Washington on business, and wishing to be present at the execution, left Alexandria for Leesburg, Va., and from that place he came here in a buggy; that he came through curiosity alone, having determined not to discuss the subject of slavery while here. He also says he was not aware that the Union had been dissolved, and was under the impression that he was still in the United States, until he reached this town. Whilst conversing with the guard in relation to the hanging of Brown, he burst into a flood of tears, and on being asked the cause of his grief, he said he had lost his father a few months ago. In appearance and conversation, he is very gentlemanly, and bears up under his confinement with patience.

MEN OF BUSINESS OBLIGED TO ABANDON THEIR BUSINESS. — *Washington, Dec. 8th.* Thirty-two gentlemen, agents of New York and Boston houses, arrived here to-day from the South, and report the feeling of indignation so great against Northerners, that they were compelled to return and abandon their business. These gentlemen have been known for years as traders in the South. They also report that Northerners of long residence in the South have been disfigured, and driven from their homes.

Eleven business men who were on their way South returned last night, after having reached a station in Virginia, being turned back by a Vigilance Committee. They say the feeling in six of the States through which they have passed is very intense against the North, and against the continuance of the Union.

THE WAY ABOLITION EMISSARIES ARE TREATED IN SOUTH-
WESTERN VIRGINIA. A philanthropic pilgrim from the land
of wooden nutmegs, supposed to be an agent of some Abolition
Aid Society or underground railroad, was arrested the other
day in the neighboring county of Pulaski, and dealt with in
the most summary manner by his captors; one of the most
influential and worthy citizens of the county acting as judge,
jury, and executioner. After ordering him to be hung by the
neck, he very coolly proceeded to execute the sentence. Having hung him up until the "vital spark" was nearly extinct,
he cut him down and gave him a breathing spell. When sufficiently restored to undergo another swinging, he was again
haltered, and suspended for a few moments. After having
undergone this process five times, (once each for old Brown,
Coppick, Cook, Stevens, and Hazlett,) he was kindly permitted to retrace his steps to a more congenial clime, but not until he had been fairly admonished that if ever caught in Virginia again, he would have to take the sixth and fatal leap.
It is said by those who witnessed the whole proceeding, that
when the fellow got loose, he ran like a quarter nag. —
Wytheville (Va.) Telegraph.

A MAN INDICTED FOR EXPRESSING SYMPATHY WITH BROWN.
— The Grand Jury of Norfolk, Va., have found a true bill
on an indictment against S. Daneburg, who keeps a clothing
and shoe store in that city, for seditious language, calculated
to incite insurrection. The *Day Book* says : —

"The first count charged him with having used the words,
'John Brown was a good man, and was fighting in a good
cause, and did nothing but what any honest man would do.'
And the second count charged that he had used the following
expressions: 'John Brown was fighting in a good cause,'
(meaning that he was fighting in the cause of the slave against
the master,) 'and that owners have no right of property in
their slaves'; and said that 'Brown did nothing but what
any other honest man would do.' Daneburg left the city a
few days ago, having an intimation that he had got himself
into trouble. His case will come on early in the present term
of the Superior Court, now in session."

A CONSERVATIVE MINISTER DRIVEN FROM NORTH CARO-
LINA. The Rev. B. C. Smith, of Prattsburgh, is sojourning
temporarily in the "Old North State," having the double
object in view of benefitting his health, and laboring in his
calling with such ability as is left to him. He went out under the auspices of the Southern Aid Society, after having
correspondence with a prominent public functionary of North
Carolina. At Washington he was warmly welcomed by Hon.
John A. Gilmer, of that State, and furnished with kindly
passports to the confidence of that gentleman's family and
friends. He carries with him the earnest hope of troops of
friends that the mild Southern skies may be beneficial to him,
and that there, as here, he may have strength to proclaim
those essential doctrines of Christianity which he so well understands, and which alone constitute "the glorious Gospel
of the blessed God."

We copy the above from the last *Advocate*. Before its
publication, the Rev. B. C. Smith had returned from the
"Old North State," without "having proclaimed" to its
citizens "those essential doctrines of Christianity which he so
well understands," and without having materially benefitted
his health. Notwithstanding he went thither under the auspices of the Southern Aid Society, and with "passports"
from Hon. John A. Gilmer, the fact that he had breathed the
air of freedom was an insuperable objection, and he was not
allowed to enter a pulpit. Learning that a Methodist brother
was in "durance vile" across the way, on suspicion of entertaining anti-slavery sentiments, the Rev. B. C. Smith bade
adieu to "mild Southern skies," and returned to his Northern home. Mr. Smith was regarded here by a portion of his
congregation as "pro-slavery," and would have been the last
man in the world to give offence to the advocates of the peculiar institution, but he has returned the victim of, if not a
firm believer in, the "irrepressible conflict."— *Northern
Christian Advocate.*

A suspicious man is in jail at Union, Monroe Co., Virginia.
He has but one arm, says he is from Baltimore, and that his
name is Nicholas Mitchell.

THE VIRGINIA FRIGHT.   The panic has seized all classes of
the people, and most exaggerated reports are in circulation.
Some think that hordes of Northerners are on their way to
invade the State which has given birth to Presidents and
statesmen.   Petersburg has been divided into patrol districts,
and fines of $25 and $50 are to be imposed upon those who
disobey orders to perform patrol duty whenever Major Daven-
port, the officer left to protect the city, may call for their services.   Seven men each from eight companies were on patrol
duty last night, and a special detachment was sent to guard
the powder magazine on the other side of the river Appo-
matox.   These warlike preparations are, of course, a serious
interruption to all business in the city, and the suspicions
which are excited by them contribute to the same result.

If five or six negroes are seen talking together, they are
speedily magnified by rumor into a hundred, armed with pitch-
forks and scythe blades.   Beggars are arrested and put into
jail, and strangers, if they happen to be poorly dressed, are accosted by the police and examined.   Two of this class, who
were found a night or two ago, had in their possession a tin
cup and ρ whiskey-flask, with a little spirits in it, supposed to
be of Northern manufacture, an old jack-knife, and a piece
of string.   They were ordered to leave the city immediately;
but before they had time to comply with the injunction, they
were again taken into custody. — *Letter from Petersburg, Va.*

In North Carolina, Rev. Alfred Vestal has been forced to
leave his work, by the spirit of violence which has recently
broken out there.   He is now in Indiana.   A Christian sister
in North Carolina writes that the immediate cause of his
leaving was his having learned that warrants for his arrest,
on charges similar to those against Mr. Worth, were issued,
both in Randolph and Guilford counties.

At Charlestown, Virginia, the military authorities not only
held possession of the telegraph, but also interfered with the
mails.   Letters directed to certain of the New York papers
were not forwarded; and packages of newspapers from New
York were suppressed.

Vigilance Committees are being organized in every county, town and village of the Commonwealth. The following preamble and resolutions, adopted at a highly respectable meeting of the citizens of the counties of Madison and Culpepper, held recently at a place called Locust Dale, will suffice to show the object of these Vigilance Committees. The sentiments they express may be esteemed a fair index of those uttered at meetings held elsewhere for a similar purpose, and, in fact, of the general sentiment of the State : —

Whereas, in view of the present troubled state of the times, and the outrageous inroad made upon our peace and happiness by recent occurrences in our midst, and in view of the fact that we have reason to believe that our country is traversed throughout its whole extent by Abolition emissaries in the guise of peddlers and venders of patent rights, quack nostrums, &c., we, a part of the citizens of Madison and Culpepper, deem it a duty to ourselves, to the welfare of our country, and more especially to the protection of our peculiar institutions, to adopt the following resolutions, to wit : —

1. That a Vigilance Committee be appointed, whose duty it shall be to examine all suspicious persons who cannot give a satisfactory account of themselves, and to dispose of said persons as may seem to them to be expedient.

2. That it be considered the duty of each member of this meeting to exercise the utmost vigilance in arresting every individual of suspicious character, and in handing him over to the Vigilance Committee, and that every citizen be requested to co-operate with them. A third resolution, naming twenty-six gentlemen as a Vigilance Committee, was then adopted.

A similar meeting was held in Luray, Page county, and a Vigilance Committee, consisting of thirty-two, appointed for the same purpose. Meetings have also been held in Rockingham, Shenandoah, Orange, and several other counties, each of which has organized its Vigilance Committee. Volunteer companies are also being rapidly organized in every town and village of the State — *Virginia correspondent of New York Herald.*

PERSONAL. Several Cincinnati ladies were travelling down the Mississippi, and while the steamer was letting off freight at a station, went ashore for a walk. Dr. Horton, the owner of the plantation, sent a negro to order them off, to which they paid no attention, when the chivalric Doctor himself informed the ladies that he " didn't want people, male or female, from so abolition a hole as Cincinnati, prowling about his premises." The ladies retired.

First be sure of public opinion before you express your own in a free country! Because he did not keep this sound maxim in mind, Mr. T. A. Salvo has had his head shaved gratis on one side, been treated to a coat of tar and feathers, ridden on a rail, and compelled to listen to a lecture. All this happened at Hamburg — not in Germany, for they are not enlightened there, but in — South Carolina. Mr. Salvo's offence was his expression of the opinion that slavery was not a good thing. Strong as were the arguments made use of to convince him of his error, we doubt if his sentiments have undergone any change. What a terrible cry there would be if a Palmetto man should be tarred and feathered in Massachusetts for saying slavery *is* a good thing! Yet the deed would be in no respect different from what has just been done in South Carolina, because a man said he thought slavery was *not* a good thing. — *Boston Traveller.*

A correspondent of the Charleston *Mercury*, writing from Blackville, in that State, after narrating the circumstance connected with the tarring of Salvo, says: " On the 14th, we sent off a foot-traveller, who was passing through the country with an air-gun, a dice-box, and some stereoscopic views; and last night we started back to Charleston a man named Jones, who came here with his wife direct from Vermont, for the professed purpose of taking ambrotypes. Having no use for such vagabond characters, when they hail from Abolition territory, we advise them to keep away."

Two persons, whose presence was considered undesirable on account of Abolitionism, were ridden on a rail at Kingstree, South Carolina, not long since. One was an old man, and the other a young man of good personal appearance. They were carried about the village, borne by negroes, and compelled to sing while travelling in this manner. They were then turned loose. They took the noon train for Charleston, but the other passengers refusing to ride with them, they were put out of the cars at St. Stephen's station.

MORE INCENDIARISM. The *States and Union* keeps up its vile and incendiary appeals against this office, in its issue of Monday, as follows: —

"The police should have a scrutinizing eye on all suspicious, evil-looking persons who may take shelter in the city. The railroad depot should be closely observed. The incendiary printing offices should be closely watched. The 'devil's den,' or Black Republican Association Lodge, should not escape attention.

"If Black Republicanism had in its service John Brown, who risked so much upon an expedition to take Harper's Ferry, what may not be undertaken with such shelter as may be afforded by the league of Black-Brown spirits who infest this community? The price of public security, like that of public liberty, is eternal vigilance." — *National Era, Wash.*

AN ABOLITIONIST CAUGHT IN ALABAMA. We heard on Saturday that an Abolitionist emissary had been detected at Prattville, in Autauga County, on the previous day, and rather summarily dealt with by the citizens of that village. He was immediately arrested and put upon his trial, which resulted in his being bound over in the sum of $10,000. It is stated that this fellow had in his possession several letters from some of Brown's men in the North, relative to the plans of that infamous band of rebellionists, and containing advice as to how he should act — what point to fix upon as head-quarters, &c. &c. He was first arrested on suspicion of being the murderer of McCrabb, and, on examination, these incendiary documents were found about his person. We hope to be able to give full particulars of this affair in our issue of Tuesday. The plot, indeed, seems to thicken. — *Montgomery Advertiser, Nov. 28th.*

The Warrentown (Va.) *Flag*, having been informed that over twenty copies of the New York *Tribune* are taken at the post-offices of Prince William county, suggests that those receiving them should not only be presented before the Grand Jury and fined heavily, but dealt with even more severely.

SENT AWAY. No less than four men, suspected of being Abolition emissaries, were arrested in our city on Friday and Saturday, examined before a committee appointed by the citizens, and finally discharged, with an injunction to leave, with their faces turned Northward — which injunction they seemed to obey, not only readily, but thankfully. We understand that there was no strong, positive evidence of very improper conduct on the part of any of them, and, therefore, we refrain from giving a description of them. It is best for all transient Northern men to have a known and honest business when they come South just now, and we do not condemn the disposition to expel them if they cannot exhibit such "credentials;" nevertheless, we trust that the people of this and every other Southern community will continue to act coolly and cautiously — that they will not inflict personal violence without sufficient proof that it is deserved — *Columbus (Ga.) Enquirer.*

Arkansas has been extending her pro-slavery courteous hospitalities to a Democratic citizen of Clark county, Ohio, who was on a visit to that State, in connection with the sale of fruit trees. He registered himself at Napoleon from Springfield, Ohio. This was enough to excite suspicion. The mob gathered, he exhibited letters from prominent Democrats of Ohio, among them Hon. W. S. Groesbeck, but these, and his tree talk, were no go. His credentials were returned, he was escorted to the boat, and the nursery agent hurried up the Mississippi as a "d—d abolitionist!"

Mr. Ashley, a Republican member of Congress from Ohio, went to Charlestown, Va., and witnessed the execution of John Brown. Some hours before the execution, he was discovered to be a spy, and he plainly avowed himself to the crowd to be a Republican member of Congress. His intrepidity alone saved his life. He was insulted, his life was threatened a hundred times, but by cool bearing, he put his panic-stricken foes to shame, and they did not venture to attack him.

THE "IRREPRESSIBLE CONFLICT" A TWO-EDGED SWORD. —
The South is laying about with its anti-abolition weapons with
such blind fury that friends as well as foes are struck down.
An incident illustrative of this recently occurred at Columbus, Mississippi. The agent of a Northern mercantile house
visiting the city was suspected of being an Abolitionist in disguise, and having left town for a day or two, Mr. James Blair
searched his trunk for proof of his treasonable character. He
found, on opening the trunk, a copy of a letter to a friend,
which commenced by saying that it was "all right with him
and the Brown family;" then Mr. Blair's excitement was
reported to have been very great, and he threw down the letter, confident that he had detected treason.

A bystander picked up the letter, and upon a further perusal, discovered that the "Brown family" in question was not
that of Osawatomie, but was the family of old Mr. and Mrs.
Brown, who had a certain daughter that had captivated the
unfortunate drummer; then followed an overhauling of the
correspondence of the unfortunate swain, which resulted in
some very interesting developments in the way of soft sentiments. At this juncture of affairs, Dr. Shepherd came up,
and pronounced the procedure an outrage; Mr. Blair replied
with a curse, saying that if he took sides with the Northern
agents, he was no better than one of them. Shepherd then
told him that he would have to answer for his remarks, or
something to that effect, and, arming himself with a walking-
stick, for a day or two was on the watch for Blair to show
himself in the streets. That individual, however, kept out of
the way until the second night after the words were passed,
when they met, and Shepherd commenced caning Blair, whereupon Blair drew a pistol, and shot him three times, Shepherd
continuing to cane him until he fell dead. Thus was the Doctor's life sacrificed to a blind rage against Abolitionists. Dr.
Shepherd formerly resided in Texas, and held the position of
Secretary of the Navy under Gen. Houston, in the time of the
Texan Republic. He was the special friend of Commodore
Moore, of the Texan Navy.

———

Two alleged Abolitionists have been arrested in Mobile,
Alabama, and compelled to give bonds or leave the State.

MORE ARRESTS AND EXPULSIONS. The Charleston *Mercury*, of the 17th ult., says that a man, supposed to be an Abolitionist, of dark complexion, with black hair and a scar over the left eye, about five feet eleven inches in height, and calling himself James W. Rivers, was taken up on the 13th by the Vigilance Committee, tarred and feathered, and the right side of his head shaven.

We learn that two men arrived in this city yesterday morning, having been dismissed from Sumter. Confident in the honesty of their intentions, and feeling innocent of any misdemeanor, they will endeavor to regain their residence at Sumter.

During last week, a few young men, in a frolicking spirit, agreed to play Vigilance Committee, and cause the first man they should meet to give a strict account of himself. They had not proceeded far ere they met a Charleston gentleman, who, surmising that nothing but sport was at the bottom of it, submitted to their catechism, and told them distinctly that he was a South Carolinian and a Charlestonian. One of the self-constituted Vigilants, in the pride of his position, hinted that the matter might be all right; but that an unprejudiced evidence, other than the examined gentleman, was necessary to satisfy him. This was too much, even for the good nature of the impressed gentleman, who squared off, and, by a well-directed blow, landed his persistent examiner in the middle of the street. As his comrades picked him up, he exclaimed, "I reckon he's a Southerner; let's go along!" This was the end of that Vigilance Committee.

Itinerant teachers, peddlers, drummers, &c., are so numerous in Frederick County, Md., that the people fear a second Harper's Ferry affair, and have set a watch over the barracks, where seven hundred stand of arms are deposited, lest they should be broken into or taken possession of.

In South Easton, Pa., on the 22d of February, an itinerant peddler of the "Life of John Brown" was treated to a dozen lashes on the back, and ordered out of town!

ANOTHER MECHANIC DRIVEN FROM THE SOUTH. Mr. Perley Seaver, of Oxford, a year ago last May, went to South Carolina to superintend a steam saw mill, his employer also being an Oxford man. By industry and economy, he accumulated sufficient funds to purchase a house, and he thought himself settled for life. Mr. Seaver, says the Worcester (Mass.) *Transcript*, was a quiet, religious man, and as there was no preaching or other religious exercises in the place, he was wont to call his neighbors together on the Sabbath to read the Bible and hear a sermon. A rumor got round the village that " Seaver preached Abolition sermons," but nothing was done about it until Saturday night, Christmas Eve. At 1 o'clock in the morning, he was waited upon by a large delegation, who, after ransacking his papers and books, and obtaining from him an admission that five negroes had attended his meetings — how many whites attended is not stated — ordered him to leave within twenty days. Seaver offered to go at once, if they would buy his place, but this they refused, and he came away within the specified time, finding it impossible to dispose of his property.

———

ARREST OF SUSPECTED EMISSARIES. A correspondent of the Baltimore *Sun*, writing from Rockville, Md., under the date of Nov. 25, says : —

" We have one of Brown's sympathizers with us, a man calling himself Wm. McDougal, or Dougal. He was committed to our jail on the 23d inst., and had a second hearing on the 24th, before Squire Braddock, of our town, after which he was recommitted, for uttering sympathy sentiments for ' Old Brown.' The language used was that he thought Brown was doing right, and that he ought to free every negro in the South. He says he was born in Franklin County, Pa., but for the last twelve or fifteen years, has been working in Maryland and Virginia. His wife and child are in Cumberland, Maryland, and his brothers and sisters live in Monroe county, Ohio. He says he had no idea of doing any harm in saying what he did. He was arrested on the Chesapeake and Ohio Canal, near Seneca. I suppose he is about 30 or 35 years of age, about 5 feet, 6 or 7 inches high, and not very stoutly made. B."

ANOTHER ALARM — TORPEDOES DISCOVERED. The Rich-mond *Enquirer* reports another important discovery : —

" Among the thousand rumors which we have heard daily of revengeful acts, as being in contemplation by the hardened sinners, the friends, admirers and abettors of Old Brown and Company, is the following :

" When all chances for making a successful rescue fail the Abolitionists, they will strive to get satisfaction for the deaths of the miserable beings at Charlestown by sending parcels of death-dealing and explosive materials to the most prominent parties in Virginia, who were in favor of the letter of the law being strictly carried out in regard to the condemned pris-oners.

" These ' *torpedoes,*' or ' *infernal machines,*' *are generally made up in most deceptive packages*, and labelled so as to pre-vent all suspicion of danger on the part of the receiver. The latter naturally undoes the package in a hurry, and, in pulling off the lid or cover, starts some concealed spring, or other ig-niting contrivance, and the whole affair explodes, with the sound and fury of a bomb-shell, dealing death and destruction around.

" Such a killing conception is truly worthy of the demons who would lend money, means and succor, to incite our South-ern slaves to rise in rebellion, with midnight dagger, poison and incendiary's torch, to destroy their owners and protectors, with our wives and children ! "

SENT OFF. We learn from a gentleman just arrived from Unionville, that the citizens of that place are exercising a commendable vigilance with regard to suspicious characters among them. At a meeting of the Town Council, on Wednes-day last, three persons, whose movements have been regarded with some suspicion, were ordered to leave the place, within twenty-four hours, or be dealt with summarily. Our inform-ant states that they complied with the order immediately, without even bidding their landlord adieu.

We also learn from the Kingstree *Star* that two printers, caught in the company of some negroes at the depot in that place, were treated to a ride on a rail, and sent out of town. — *Columbia (S. C.) Guardian.*

A FULMINATION FROM VIRGINIA. The Richmond *Whig* publishes the following amiable exhortation: —

BUCKINGHAM, Wednesday, Nov. 9, 1859.

TO THE EDITOR OF THE WHIG: — In yesterday's *Whig*, I notice a paragraph, about eight lines in length, which I do think is worth all that I have seen about Harper's Ferry altogether. You have hit the nail exactly on the head! The article is headed " Abolition Emissaries," and the part which pleases us most is this:

" The truth is, we have no longer any use for the vagabond tourists or itinerant peddlers, of unknown characters, who have heretofore found free course among us. And it becomes our citizens to hold all such to account."

Now, that's sense. Them's my sentiments, and I go in for getting rid of the whole crew. A plague upon their whole mas! Don't encourage them; don't buy any thing from them; don't employ them in any way — I mean the whole of them, of every description, style, caste and color. If they don't leave, why, starve them out! Any thing, any way to get rid of them. Amen!

A SUBSCRIBER.

Two young men (brothers) took letters from —— ——, a noted Democrat of Woodstock, Connecticut, to Governor Letcher, of Virginia, stating that they were all right, *i. e.*, " sound on the goose " in regard to slavery. But, (mark this!) they were mechanics — carpenters — and, of course, " had no rights that slaveholders were bound to respect"; consequently, they were watched in words and actions. One day, some of the butterfly troops of Virginia were on parade, and a remark was made by one of the brothers that they were a fine-looking set of men! The other replied, Yes, they were; but twenty Yankees would drive them all into the swamp; which observation was overheard by a slaveholder, who instantly had the mob upon them, and they barely escaped with their lives, glad to get home to old Woodstock — changed in their views in regard to the peculiar institution and Democracy. — *Correspondent of the Boston Liberator.*

Two Trenton Mechanics Driven from Virginia. Two
tinsmiths of Trenton, who had been hired to go to the vicinity
of Charlestown, Va., to do some roofing, returned a few days
ago, having been prevented from doing their work, and driven
by threats of arrest to leave the place. An account of the
affair. which appears to be authentic, is as follows : —
   " A wealthy gentleman of New Jersey, understood to be a
Mr. H. J. Garrison, formerly a dry goods merchant at Trenton, who removed to a locality near Charlestown in 1854, or
about that time, having concluded to remain permanently at
the latter place, had partly built a house, which he designed
to cover with a metallic roof. Preferring the work of Northern mechanics, or finding it impracticable to get it done without incurring the considerable expense of bringing them so
great a distance, he came on to Trenton and engaged two tin-
workers, who had been employed in the hardware establishment of G. Brearly & Co., of that city. Taking them with
him, he returned to his Southern home, and the work was
about being commenced. But the Virginians had no idea of
allowing any such proceeding ; nobody knew but that this was
a contrivance of the Abolitionists — at any rate, it could not
be permitted. So they threatened the tin-workers they would
arrest them and deal summarily with them, if they did not
forthwith depart, and the mechanics, to avoid trouble, concluded to go home. Their employer was at the same time
informed that his house might remain for ever uncovered, if
he could not get it roofed without sending to the North for
Abolitionists to do the work."

Not a Safe Place for Yankees. On the day that John
Brown was in possession of Harper's Ferry, the Superintendent of the Harper's Ferry Armory was in Springfield, Mass.,
to get a new master armorer for that establishment, and engaged Mr. Salmon Adams, the clerk and assistant of the master armorer at the Government shops in Springfield. But
since he has got home, he writes back cancelling the engagement, for the reason that the people there are so exasperated
with the Yankees, that they would not stand one of them in
the place of master armorer. They would butcher him, he
says, should Mr. Adams come on and take the place !

EXCITEMENT IN TALBOT COUNTY, MD. On Sunday last, an incendiary letter was picked up in St. Michael's, which purports to give the outlines of an extended insurrectionary movement in Maryland and Virginia. It states the very improbable fact, that over 12,000 men are engaged in the crusade, who can instantly recognize each other by a look in the eyes whenever they meet. The plot contemplates the capture of the city of Baltimore, by the aid of 40,000 men from the North, the time to be fixed by a State Convention of the crusaders, to be held in this city. The name and date of the letter were both torn off. This ridiculous document created great excitement among the good people of Talbot. Patrols were immediately formed in the St. Michael's district, and a strong guard placed in Easton on Sunday night. A public meeting of the citizens of the county took place in the courthouse at Easton, yesterday afternoon, to take into consideration the existing state of affairs, but we have not learned the result of their deliberations. — *Baltimore Republican, November* 30.

Col. S. A. Cooley, of this city, was in Charlestown, Va., last week. Mr. Penfield, agent of Sharpe's Rifle Company, was also there. Both were placed under arrest, but were treated kindly. Mr. Penfield showed a letter of introduction from the Secretary of War, Mr. Floyd. Col. Cooley protested that he was no Abolitionist. But all availed nothing. The officer said, "Gentlemen, we have no reason to believe that either of you meditate harm; but the authorities have directed that the movements of all strangers shall be guarded; this is absolutely necessary for our safety; persons pretending to be friendly have been among us for some time, and our horses and cattle have been poisoned at night; our barns and sheds and haystacks have been destroyed by fire; the property of some of the jurors in John Brown's case has been burnt by incendiaries; we have only stopped these alarming proceedings by the most decided action in permitting no strangers to be staying about here in idleness." Messrs. Cooley and Penfield, seeing the absolute necessity for the regulations which had been established, then left the place. — *Hartford Times, Dec. 14th.*

A REWARD OFFERED FOR THE HEAD OF MR. GIDDINGS. — The following advertisement appears in the Richmond *Whig*:

Ten Thousand Dollars Reward. — Joshua R. Giddings, having openly declared himself a *traitor* in a lecture at Philadelphia, on the 28th of October, and there being no process, strange to say, by which he can be brought to justice, I propose to be one of one hundred to raise $10,000 for his safe delivery in Richmond, or $5,000 for the production of his head. I do not regard this proposition, extraordinary as it may at first seem, either *unjust or unmerciful.* The law of God and the Constitution of his country both condemn him to death.

For satisfactory reasons, I withhold my name from the public, but it is in the hands of the editor of the Richmond *Whig.* There will be no difficulty, I am sure, in raising the $10,000, upon a reasonable prospect of getting the said Giddings to this city.

Richmond, Nov. 1, 1859.

————

The Providence *Journal* says: — "We lately mentioned that a twelve pound cannon ball had been found here in a bale of cotton, and we then took occasion to remark, that the substitution of iron for sand as an article to increase the weight of the bale showed a slight moral improvement in the dishonest packers. But something worse even than sand has been found in a bale which recently arrived. That is, lucifer matches. They were in a pine box, which was partially broken, so that they could not fail to ignite in passing through the picker. Had they not been accidentally discovered, they might have caused the destruction of one of the most valuable mills in this State."

————

A dentist, who has advertised himself for the last eighteen months in Charleston, S. C., as desiring to cure tooth-ache without pain, was waited upon, on the 17th ult., by a committee, who were fortified by the oaths of two reliable citizens before a magistrate, and notified that, considering his avowed Abolitionism, he must select another residence. He left.

IN A DILEMMA.   A young gentleman, whose parents reside in a neighboring county in an adjoining State, is just now in rather an unpleasant dilemma in Kentucky, the result of the jealousy induced by the persistent attempts of Abolitionists to excite a servile insurrection, which culminated by the invasion at Harper's Ferry.   The facts came to our knowledge to-day, and are vouched for by men of veracity, though the name of the young man was not given.   He was, it seems, employed as a teacher, and was in the full tide of success, and quite popular among the patrons of his school, until the fact became known that he frequently received letters from Oberlin, about which he was extremely shy.   The excitement about the Harper's Ferry invasion, and rumors of contemplated attempts in Kentucky, awakened so much suspicion, that the young man was finally taken into custody, and placed in the hands of a committee of citizens to investigate his case, about which suspicion was very much increased upon his refusal to divulge the nature of his correspondence with Oberlin. — *Adrian (Mich.) paper.*

———

LITERATURE IN LEECHVILLE.   Somewhere down in the tar and rosin State is a shambling sort of a hamlet called Leechville.   They have a post-office in Leechville.   The man who overhauls the mails at this out-of-the-way spot is one Augustus Latham.   From the Blue Book, it appears that the annual receipts of this post-office are thirty-one dollars, whereof Latham pockets twenty-one for his salary, leaving ten to replenish the Federal Treasury, which probably pays some Democratic contractor a hundred dollars per annum for going off the main road in search of Leechville, and stopping long enough for the contractor's horse to catch breath, and the contractor's driver to imbibe a draught of whiskey, while Latham peers into the half-dozen letters and newspapers, more or less, in the mail bag.   One would suppose that the arrival in this desolate locality of a half-dozen speeches, bearing the frank of some U. S. Senator, would be hailed as a godsend, even if only for the novelty of the thing.   It seems that there is a resident in Leechville, permanent or temporary, who is pursuing knowledge under difficulties — one Thomas Dunbar, the

6*

senior of that name.   Hearing (we confess we are at a loss to
guess how) that Senator Wilson had delivered a speech exposing the Disunion schemes of the Democracy, Mr. Dunbar
wrote to that gentleman, requesting him to send him two or
three copies of that speech; which, of course, Mr. Wilson
did.   The return mail brings to the Senator a missive from
Mr. Holt's man Latham.   We print it as an average speci-
men of Southern respect for law, Southern manners and Southern grammar : —

                                "LEECHVILLE Feb 16 1860.
  "SIR Your speeches and your Black Republican friends cannot circulate
your Abolition speeches through this Post office so you need not send any
more to Thomas Dunbar senr
        "Yours &c   AUGUSTUS LATHAM P M"

Latham's orthography is inimitable; so, in that particular,
we fall back upon Webster.

In all seriousness, there has been quite enough of this sort
of mail robbery under the rule of Mr. Holt.   If he does n't
stop it promptly and peremptorily, he should be impeached.
Such creatures as this Latham should be dismissed instanter.
If Mr. Holt, on due notice, refuses to have this done, then
the House of Representatives should immediately take the
initial step toward degrading him from office. — *New York
Tribune.*

Dr. Mulroe, of South Carolina, the owner of two planta-
tions, and negroes sufficient to work them, was arrested a few
days ago, as a suspicious character, by a Vigilance Committee, in Eufala, Ala.   The Doctor was peddling ploughs, and
it was hard to believe that so wealthy a man would turn
" travelling Yankee."   A friend, who knew the Doctor at
home, happened to be in town, however, and hearing of the
difficulty he was in, went to the place where the committee
were trying him, and when he entered, and found Dr. M. occupying a chair, and undergoing an examination, under such
peculiar circumstances, he was so astonished that he exclaimed,
" Why, Dr. Mulroe!" and burst out in a loud laugh, while
the Doctor, overcome with his feelings, burst into tears, and
the sympathy was so intense, that the whole committee were
soon in tears!   As a finale, all pledged themselves to sell as
many ploughs as they could.

THE EXCITEMENT AGAINST NORTHERN MEN IN VIRGINIA.—
The Richmond correspondent of the New York *Herald*, writing
on the 18th, says:—

"A gentleman from Baltimore, who was on his way South
upon a tour for the benefit of his health, informed me, last
evening, that however great might be the advantages of the
trip, he would forego it, sooner than submit to the suspicions
and scrutinies of which he was the object at various points
upon his passage through Virginia. He travell:d through
some portions of the interior of the Commonwealth, before
reaching here. I know an instance in which the presentation
of a Massachusetts bank note at a tavern in the country, by a
gentleman who resides in Virginia, and is sound upon the
State, was nearly subjecting him to serious indignities and in-
conveniences. His recognition by a gentleman of the locality,
as he emerged from the tavern, was the only thing that saved
him from a disagreeable overhauling. The gentleman assured
me that he was well armed, and determined that the first man
who laid hands upon him should die. I have had myself some
little experience in this sort of treatment, and I can therefore
appreciate its disadvantages. While standing in the hall of
a hotel, in North Carolina, some year or two ago, awaiting
the meeting of an assembly whose proceedings I had gone to
report for the *Herald*, I was rudely seized by two ruffians,
who planted themselves on each side of me, and carried me
into the street, there to ascertain what my purpose in coming
to town was, and to administer due punishment, if it was not
in keeping with their views. By this time, we were approached
by several persons, amongst whom, most fortunately for me,
was a distinguished gentleman of that State, who instantly
recognized me. The observance of the recognition by these
ruffians caused them immediately to release me. Being then
without any means of defence, I was forced to submit to this
indignity."

———

The surest way, and perhaps the only way, to prevent such
resorts to that justly reprobated code — lynch law — is, for
those philanthropists who *cannot* restrain the expression of
their anti-slavery sentiments, to leave the benighted communities of the South, and make their homes in more congenial
regions. — *Savannah News.*

There is a College at Roanoke, Va., and, of course, its students had to improve John Brown's raid. 'Twas thus they did it, on the 3d of December : —

"Forasmuch, as the sacred soil of Virginia has been invaded, her citizens incarcerated, and innocent blood shed by a band of monomaniac fanatics, instigated to the desperate deed by individuals beyond the reach of law and justice, therefore,

"Resolved, 1st, That we, the students of Roanoke College, under the protection of the laws of Virginia, do express our sentiments towards Wm. H. Seward, Joshua R. Giddings, and Wendell Phillips, by casting upon them the infamous stigma of burning them in effigy.

"Resolved, 2d, That we fire a cannon as each image is consumed by the flames, and give three cheers for our intrepid, indefatigable, vigilant Governor, Henry A. Wise.

"Resolved, 3d, That we shall ever be ready to enlist under the standard of our State, to defend Virginia and her rights, under all emergencies."

JOHN BROWN IN FLORIDA. A gentleman, who is spending the winter in Florida for the benefit of his health, writes : —

"The news of the John Brown affair reached Florida before we did, and a party of chivalrous citizens had an indignation meeting, and threatened to tar and feather any Abolitionist who might venture among them. I understood from one of the residents of the place, that not one of the indignant citizens aforesaid owned a slave, or had money enough to buy one. They appointed a committee to wait on a poor Jersey minister, half dead with bronchitis, but the only thing they could find against him was, that he had been seen to shake hands with a nigger, so they only warned him."

A book agent, named Day, who made his appearance in the village yesterday afternoon, was ordered to leave on the one one o'clock train for Columbia. Before the arrival of the cars, however, he was seen giving leg bail along the railroad, in the direction of Charleston. — *Orangeburg* (*S. C.*) *Southron.*

"Let us prepare for disunion; not precipitate it. Between this and the 4th of March, 1861, the Union cannot harm us. In the meanwhile, let us enact laws of retaliation and non-intercourse, and establish a direct trade, and, consequently, friendly relations, with Europe. Let us charge heavy license for the sale of all goods from the North, whether produced there, or imported from abroad; let us send our cotton, rice and tobacco, directly to Europe; let us establish a stricter espionage over all visitors from the North, and a stricter espionage over all Virginians who deal or associate with them.

"We may treat such Northerners as we please as persons of *ill fame*, improper company for Virginians, and recognize, fine and imprison *our own citizens*, who deal or associate with them. Thus we might expel all the itinerant quacks and peddlers and teachers from the most inimical Northern States, —and from all of those States, if experience proved it necessary to our safety. We might also punish our citizens who shipped grain by Yankee vessels, or procured goods of any sort by them.

"The election of a Black Republican as President in 1860, unless that party adopts new leaders and a new platform, will render disunion inevitable on the 4th of March, 1861. We should delay it until that time, preparing for its consequences."
—*Richmond Enquirer*.

———

The Cincinnati *Commercial* states that anonymous letters in mourning envelopes are being sent through the Newport (Ky.) post-office, to Republican residents of that town, warning them to take their leave of the soil of Kentucky. Mr. J. R. Whittemore, a gentleman who resides in Newport, and does business in Cincinnati, recently received notice to leave, on or before the first day of December, 1859.

Four individuals, who were regarded as "rather noxious to the community," have recently been ordered to leave Orangeburg, S. C. The first was a school teacher, a young man calling himself D. Heagle, from New York. The next were two young men, house painters, one by the name of Mahon, who also hailed from the State of New York, and the other, who signed his name as Clarkson, from North Carolina. The fourth was a book agent, named Day. Each was compelled to take the first train which left town after the warning.

A KENTUCKY SYMPATHIZER IN TROUBLE. The Cincinnati *Commercial*, of Nov. 29, has the following: —

"We learn that a man by the name of Brown, late a conductor on the Lexington and Danville Railroad, happening to be in May's grocery in Lexington, last week, was bantered by the proprietor on his name, and asked whether he was ' any relation of old Osawatomie.' He replied that he was not, but took occasion to say that he endorsed his sentiments as to slavery. Thereupon the bystanders put him out of doors by violence. Shortly after, he was called on by some pretended friends, who invited him to go to Beard's stable, in Lexington, which he did, and there found a lot of men, who demanded that he should repeat what he had said about slavery. On doing so, the crowd became very much excited, and told him he had better leave Lexington, and the State.

"We are also told that he received an anonymous letter, signed, ' Many Citizens,' warning him to leave within three days, with a threat of summary measures being used to eject him, if he failed to comply. He left and came to Covington, on Saturday, where he met some of the employees of the railroad, who pretended to sympathize with him, but soon advised him not to stay longer in Kentucky.

"He has left for the West, although he would have preferred remaining in Kentucky, had it not been for this intolerant and persecuting spirit. Brown is spoken of by the Superintendent of the Lexington and Danville Railroad, as a sober intelligent and steady man."

AN ABOLITIONIST ARRAIGNED. The Charlotte (N. C.) *Carolina Bulletin* says: "We learn that on yesterday, before the county court, now in session, a Mr. Franklin Davis, residing in Farrelltown, about ten miles north of Charlotte, sitting as grand juryman, was, on motion of Solicitor D. B. Rea, expelled from the jury, for having expressed sentiments in opposition to the institution of slavery, and he was immediately bound over in the penal sum of one thousand dollars for his appearance at the next sitting of the Superior Court. The facts will all appear at the trial in May next. We take great pleasure in commending Mr. Rea for the prompt and faithful manner in which he has discharged his duty.

EXCITEMENT AT ABBEVILLE, MISSISSIPPI. The Oxford *Mercury* of Thursday, Jan. 24th, says : —

"Considerable excitement was produced in our neighboring town of Abbeville, last Sunday and Monday, by a gang of ten peddlers. Some stories represent them to us as having been Irish or German, and others that they were Abolitionists, endeavoring to stir up an insurrection. The neighborhood became greatly alarmed when they appeared, as so many of that kind of traders do not often travel together. They were, the whole ten, arrested on Monday, and taken to Abbeville and examined, but no proof was elicited against them, except that several were operating without license. They were ordered to leave the State within a given time.

ONE OF BROWN'S MAP MEN. A book peddler, named Albritton, was arrested in Marion, Ala., on the 3d inst. The *American* says : " He was arrested about 8 o'clock this morning, and carried to Cahaba, where, it is reported, they have the documents showing him to be one of the original men to be stationed on the line of the published Brown Map. We learn from Marshal Curtis, that there is sufficient proof, found in the prisoner's trunk, to convict him, beyond a shadow of a doubt, of being an emissary. If so, the Lord have mercy on his soul (?), for we know the people of Cahaba well enough to feel confident that they will give him full justice, terrible as it may be." — *Richmond Dispatch*.

A negro barber, named Wilson, went, a few days since, from his home in Chattanooga to Knoxville, Tenn., to make a few purchases. He was followed closely and keenly watched by two men of stern visage, one of whom finally drew a fearful knife, and rushed at him, exclaiming, " You're Fred Douglass! " In peril of his life, Wilson took to his heels, hotly pursued by a constantly increasing rabble, and barely escaping a terrible fate by dodging behind a fence and permitting his followers to pass by. He went home by the first train. The next morning, the two gentlemen addressed the Mayor for papers for the arrest of Fred. Douglass.

A POLITICAL REFUGEE. — IS THIS A FREE COUNTRY?   A
gentleman of good address, bearing the evidences of sincerity
and respectability, called upon us yesterday, saying that he
was an exile from Kentucky.   His name is E. J. Dean, and
his story is as follows : —

"I have been a resident of Kentucky for the last seven
years, all of which time I have been engaged in teaching.
Latterly, say since September, I have been living near Richmond, the county seat of Madison county, where I had a
school, in which I supposed I gave my patrons good satisfaction.   I do not know that during the whole time that I lived
in the State, I ever said a single word in condemnation of
slavery.   Certainly I have never been a brawler about that
or any other political matter.   To the best of my ability, I
discharged the duties which I had undertaken for pay ; and
I declare that never have I tampered with any slave or in any
way attempted to make a negro dissatisfied with his lot.
What then was my surprise, on Saturday morning last, to receive from a man who represented himself as the chairman of
the County Vigilance Committee, a warning to immediately
give up my employment and quit the State.   In answer to
my inquiry — 'Of what crime am I accused, that I should be
punished thus?' I had only this answer, 'None, only that
you are a d——d Abolitionist!'   Pleading my inability to
settle my little affairs in five minutes' time, I was graciously
permitted to remain in Richmond until Monday, when, in
obedience to the mandate which I was not at liberty to disobey, without bringing upon myself great indignity and peril,
I set out, and arrived here this morning.   This is a plain and
perfectly truthful account of my expulsion, and, so far as I
have been informed, of the causes which led thereto.   In conclusion, I have only this inquiry to make — Is this a free
country?   If so, where and what is despotism?"

Madison is one of the wealthiest, most populous and civil-
ized counties in Kentucky, but mob law is administered there
with a degree of vigor that is without parallel in all the United States.   From that county, Rev. John G. Fee and his associates — twenty-eight in all — as peaceable, orderly, industrious, Christian men and women as there are in Kentucky —
were driven out.   In that county, C. M. Clay — brave Cas-

sius — has been subjected to dangers which have more than once put his life in peril, and to a series of petty annoyances which have for years made that life a perpetual torture. The people of Madison are naturally kind and hospitable; but the majority are possessed of that purely American devil — the intolerant, rampant, persecuting spirit of slavery; and under its influence, all within its reach are subjected to a despotism, compared with which the rule of King Bomba at Naples was a government of which his subjects might be proud.

Well may Mr. Dean ask — " Is this a free country ? " — *Chicago Press and Tribune.*

HOW THE SOUTH RESPECTS THE CONSTITUTION. An ebullition of Southern chivalry was witnessed at Demossville, Pendleton county, on Saturday last, which resulted in the driving away of a peaceable citizen, for no other crime than possessing convictions, and having the manhood to express them.

According to Mr. Payne's version of the singular proceeding, he was at the depot when the cars were detained by an accident, a few days since, when a gentleman from Covington approached him, and questioned him as to his politics. Mr. Payne replied that he was a Republican. " Of what kind ? " continued his interrogator. " One of the blackest," was the reply. During this conversation, several of Mr. P.'s friends were present, and the matter rested until Saturday morning, when he received the following notice, handed him by Dr. Cummins : —

DEMOSSVILLE, KY., Dec. 10, 1859.

MR. CHARLES PAYNE — *Dear Sir :* — You having declared yourself an Abolitionist of the blackest character, we give you the limit of twenty minutes to leave this town ; if not, you will be dealt with as we think proper.

CITIZENS OF DEMOSSVILLE,
Pendleton Co., Ky.

A large and excited mob gathered around at the same time, and he was compelled to leave, in obedience to the warning. He has long been known as a Republican, and was the candidate of that party for Congress, two years ago. He has a family, who are yet in Demossville. He purposes returning home in a day or two, there to await the progress of the " irrepressible conflict." — *Cincinnati Commercial.*

ARREST AND IMPRISONMENT OF A KENTUCKY PIONEER IN
VIRGINIA. We received a visit, yesterday, from a gray-
haired Kentuckian, just from the "inhospitable shores" of
Virginia, where he has been incarcerated in jail for two weeks,
for having the presumption to be an American citizen, and
attempting to cross the State by way of the Baltimore and
Ohio Railroad. The old gentleman is a citizen of Oldham
county, Ky., — 73 years of age, — had been on to Washington to see about some land, which fell to him under the act of
Congress making provision for the soldiers of 1812, and on
his return, was seized at Martinsburg (as the train West
stopped at that place) by the vigilant . .itary stationed at
that place, and incarcerated in the jail. He was suspected of
having conceived the "deep design" of rescuing "Old Osawatomie" Brown, and accordingly, this regiment of soldiery,
aided by two or three "peace officers," instituted a vigilant
search of the old man's wardrobe. Each boot-leg, in the heated
imagination of the Virginians, contained a knife or pike, and
every pocket a revolver. The only article that was left him
was a cake of soap, which he had thoughtfully provided himself with, having been duly advised of the impurity of the
Federal city.

He remained in jail two weeks, and on the 2d of December,
after the last ghost of fear of a rescue of old John Brown —
that is to say, after the hour of 11 o'clock and 15 minutes,
A. M. — he was released, first being graciously furnished with
a pass, of which the following is a verbatim copy : —

MARTINSBURG, Dec. 2d, 1859.

To Capt. of any patrol or military company *in Virginia* :
You will pass James C. Gardner through the State of Virginia without
molestation. He has been under arrest here for two weeks, and is *all right*.
He was discharged this morning, by order of the Commandant of the bat-
talion stationed at this point.

GEO. H. MURPHY,

Attorney for the Commonwealth for Berkley Co.

How the blood in the veins of this pioneer on the "Dark
and Bloody Ground" boiled at such indignity, those who still
have faith in the existence of chivalry, generosity, and honesty of purpose, can best imagine. The old gentleman arrived
in our city last evening. Through the kindness of the officers
of the Ohio and Mississippi Railroad, he has been furnished
with a pass over the road to Louisvillle, for which place he
will depart this morning. — *Cincinnati Gazette.*

INCENDIARY DOCUMENTS IN VIRGINIA. In our last paper, under the head of "Political and Personal," we briefly noticed the arrest of John H. Gargas and Thomas Cruix, in Fairfax County, Virginia, charged with circulating incendiary documents, Helper's book particularly. They were held to bail in large sums to answer at court. We learn from the last number of the Fairfax *News*, that Mr. Gargas was tried for the offence before a "called court," consisting of five justices. It appears that Mr. Gargas is a Postmaster in Fairfax county, and handed out one of Helper's books, received by mail, to a citizen of the neighborhood, being of course ignorant of what it was. This coming to the ears of the Virginians, they determined to act at once in the spirit of Postmaster General Holt's decision, authorizing the robbery of the mails. However, at the trial, after hearing the testimony, the court concluded to discharge Mr. Gargas. Mr. G. is nearly connected with the Geil and Gargas families, living near Doylestown, being a nephew of Abraham Gargas, of Warrington. His father moved to Fairfax county many years ago, and held a post-office, in which he was succeeded by his son. The other suspected person, Mr. Cruix, who was held in $2,500 to appear at court, has forfeited his bond by making his escape from the Commonwealth. — *Bucks County (Pa.) Intelligencer.*

———

SERGEANT BIRNEY DRIVEN OUT OF THE SOUTH. The Virginia panic, since the shooting of the cow, seems to have extended into other States. Sergeant Birney, whose career in this city, as a policeman, was brought to a termination some months since, has just arrived on the Columbia, from Charleston.

It seems that the sergeant has been pursuing the business of a merchant, in the State of Georgia, and that, since John Brown's capture of Harper's Ferry, the people of his neighborhood have been coasting about to discover any enemies lurking in among them, and suspicion fell upon the sergeant. He was questioned, and, his answers not proving satisfactory to his inquisitors, he was notified to leave. Our informant states that the alternative was a coat of tar and feathers. —*Evening Post.*

Gov. Wise Warns the South to Rouse— Yankee Peddlers, &c. The following brief letter from Gov. Wise shows what he considers the necessity of the times. We learn that very stringent measures have been adopted in South Carolina, Alabama, and in some portions of our State, against peddlers, showmen and others, who are reasonably suspected of hostility to our institutions. Scarcely a day passes, that we do not hear of some itinerant, unable to prove himself to be of reliable character, having been expelled from Southern communities. Here is the letter of the Virginia Governor : —

RICHMOND, Va., Nov. 25th, 1859.

My Dear Sir : — I have time only to acknowledge yours. Say to your father, and all others, that there are serious times here. We are arming, and have need to do so; and the Southern States all had better be rousing. Drive out peddlers and schoolmasters (not *well* known) from Yankeedom.

Yours, &c.,

HENRY A. WISE.

William Scott, Esq.

— *Atlanta (Ga.) News.*

As an illustration of the annoyance and persecution to which strangers are subjected in the sacred district of Virginia, it is stated that a Mr. Charles Grattan, of Easton, Md., hired a house and shop at Harper's Ferry, and he went there with his wife and family, and with goods to open a millinery shop. On his arrival, he was dragged at once to the arsenal, and kept in custody, and was subjected to such annoyances for several days, that he concluded Harper's Ferry was not a pleasant place to live in, and packed up his goods again and retreated back to Easton, cursing the stupidity and cowardice of the Virginians.

The Columbus (Geo.) *Sun* mentions the arrest, in that city, of Wm. Scott, a member of the firm of Charles Scott & Co., dealers in embroideries, linens, &c., New York. An open expression of sympathy for " Old Brown," and the possession of Beecher's incendiary sermons, were the occasion of the arrest. He received " notice to quit," and took his departure by the first train.

The Norristown (Pa.) *Republican* says:—"Christian Stout, a good Democrat, long a resident of Upper Dublin, and for a year or two of Plymouth township, removed to Maryland a few years ago, to work a farm for Wm. Earnest, Hon. John McNair, and others, and has resided there ever since. About two weeks ago, he appeared amongst us again, and informed us that he was a fugitive from his home. He says that a short time after the opening of Congress, and the introduction of Clark's resolution, a wealthy Englishman, his neighbor, handed him Helper's book to read. He read it, and then seeing his neighbor, he told him that he was done with it, and desired him to take it; but he said, 'No, never mind giving it to me, hand it to one of your neighbors.' He did so, and shortly afterwards the Englishman was arrested, as were some others. He was then informed that the slaveholders had sixty-two names on their paper of persons who were to be arrested for circulating Helper's book, uttering Abolition sentiments, and sympathizing with Brown. As his name was among the proscribed, he suddenly left for Pennsylvania. The Englishman was bailed in the sum of $2,500, and immediately left for New York, intending to forfeit the bail, and abandon the State. Before Stout left, he consulted a lawyer, who told him that although they might perhaps not convict him, they would probably keep him in jail a year or two, and put him to much cost, so he concluded he had better leave. He is now waiting the result of the trial of others."

A SOUTHERN OPINION OF THE REV. MR. SPURGEON. A newspaper published at Jacksonville, Florida, has a very savage attack upon the New York publishers of Mr. Spurgeon's works, apropos to the statement that "they stand ready to publish any thing that he may say on the subject of slavery." The following language, which is more forcible than elegant, is applied to Mr. Spurgeon and his publishers:—"If Messrs. ——— intend to publish the insane conceits of a beef-eating, puffed-up, vain, over-righteous, pharisaical, English, blab-mouth, ranting preacher of doctrine not found in the Bible, and worse, if possible, than the infamous book of Helper, then we think the South should know it, and bestow their patronage accordingly."

The Harper's Ferry raid demonstrates the necessity of the Northern people, in a body, and with one voice, putting down and crushing out such miserable, incendiary Abolition wretches as Giddings, Garrison, Fred. Douglass, Wendell Phillips, Seward, Wilson and Sumner. These are all schemers and conspirators against the peace of the Union.

All the powers of the Federal Government and the Government of Virginia should be employed in bringing them to a speedy justice. If there is evidence showing the complicity of Giddings, Douglass, or Thayer, or any other person in this affair, let them be arrested, tried and convicted, and punished.

As to the prisoners who were caught in the act, let them be hung, and that forthwith. There should be no temporizing and no fiddling on the part either of the President or of Governor Wise. The insurgents are nothing more nor less than pirates and murderers, entitled to none of the courtesies of war nor clemencies of law. Immediate shooting or hanging, without trial, is the punishment they merit, and the only punishment which will have the desired effect, either at the North or the South. In regard to such offenders, a just and safe principle is to hang them, and try them afterwards. — *Richmond Whig.*

The Staunton *Virginian* tells this story : — " One of our townsmen, Mr. George W. Dilliard, was involved in great danger at Harper's Ferry. He had gone there on business on the day after the capture of Old Brown and his party, and in walking along in the vicinity of the Ferry, enjoying the splendid scenery, with one of the pikes in his hand, and two or three blank commissions in his pocket, taken from the insurgents, and which Gov. Wise had given him the day before, he was pursued and captured by a party who were hunting for Cook. Mr. Dilliard was immediately charged with being one of Cook's men ; the pike was satisfactory evidence, and the cry was raised of 'shoot him ! shoot him !' and several loaded guns were pointed at his breast. Fortunately, Mr. Dilliard retained his self-possession so well that the party at last yielded to his request that he should be taken to the Superintendent at the Ferry, and there be permitted to prove his innocence. Mr. Dilliard said it was about the most trying half hour or more he ever spent.

The Charleston *Mercury*, of Tuesday, says that two Abolitionists left town on that day for the North, by steamer. One of them was taken in charge several weeks since, and has been earning his living for a month, by cracking stones for the city, agreeable to sentence imposed by the Mayor. He has acquired his trade, and leaves without a single regret. The other was received from Georgetown, where he had expressed obnoxious sentiments.

We learn from the Auburn *Signal*, that some short time ago, near Society Hill, Macon County, Alabama, a man named L. Stearns, claiming to be from Montgomery, was caught tampering with a Mr. Richardson's negroes. He was driven off, and a party of citizens caught and whipped him. Two or three nights afterwards, Mr. Richardson had a lot of cotton set on fire.

ABOLITIONISTS. As it is becoming evident that we have numerous Abolitionists in our midst, tampering with our slaves, it will behoove the planters to be strict with their servants, and not allow them too much latitude during the coming holidays. We are not alarmists, and would not create unnecessary excitement, but we warn the people to be on the alert, and hope that " a word to the wise will be sufficient." — *Vicksburg (Miss.) Southern Sun, Nov.* 22.

The *Western Christian Advocate* publishes the following from a Postmaster in Virginia : —

WAYNE, C. H. Va. Feb. 28, 1860.

To the Editor of the Western Chreston Advocate.

Sir you will Please Discontinue sending your paper to this office as it has bin found to contain incindary matter, and burnt. Yours &c

J. M. FERGUSON.

The porter of the steamship Marion, named Francis Mitchell, has been tried at Charleston, S. C., for aiding a slave in trying to escape, found guilty, and sentenced to be hanged !

A NEW YORK CAPTAIN FINED. The Richmond *Enquirer*, of Nov. 30, says: "The schooner L. Waterbury, Capt. S. A. Swinnerton, of New York, last July violated the inspection laws of Virginia, and escaped, doubtless believing inspection laws were the greatest of humbugs. She returned to our port last week, when that ever-vigilant Yankee-hunter, W. H. Parker, Chief Inspector, pounced upon the L. Waterbury, at this port, and her captain was compelled to pay $528 fine. The L. Waterbury's cargo was about $750 in lumber from Florida. Rather an unprofitable voyage for an " enterprising" Yankee.

"This, added to the previous fine, swells the amount to $3,000, besides the costs, recovered since last October, for violations of Inspection laws."

A letter from a Boston gentleman who has gone South for his health, states that on the first day out from Washington, he had a pistol held to his head, and that he was dogged by four Southern men for hundreds of miles, annoyed and insulted until he challenged the whole crowd of them to fight him, whereupon they backed out. All his newspapers from Boston have been withheld from him, and his letters have been broken open before they reached the post-office to which they were sent.

LOUISVILLE, March 27th.

A man named Hanson, who was recently expelled from Berea, Madison county, Ky., with J. G. Fee, returned to Berea, whereupon a committee waited upon him, for the purpose of again ordering him from the county. Hanson, with twenty-five or thirty associates, armed with rifles, fired upon the committee, but without injuring any one. Hanson's party then retreated, and barricaded themselves in a house. The committee, which is composed of twenty-five or thirty men, are armed with revolvers.

www.ingramcontent.com/pod-product-compliance
Lightning Source LLC
Chambersburg PA
CBHW031123020726
47495CB00007B/2317